WAR OF THE HOUNDS

WAR OF THE HOUNDS

DAVID HOPKINS

SEVEN COINS MEDIA

War of the Hounds

© 2024 David Hopkins

All right reserved. *Liber pertinet ad scriptor.*

Published by Seven Coins Media | sevencoins.media

This book is a work of fiction. All names, characters, places, and events are a product of the author's imagination and are used fictitiously Any resemblance to real people, alive or dead, or to businesses, companies, events, institutions, or locales is purely coincidental.

No part of this book may be used or reproduced in any manner without written permission except in the case of brief quotations in articles or reviews.

"Aubec Skarsol" created by Michael Brown. "Grimni" created by Ashley Georgakopoulos. Used with permission.

Developmental Editor: Holly Lyn Walrath

Copy Editors: Kara Robinson and Tricia Klapprodt

Cover Art: Daniel Irving Decena | @thepenslinger

Cover Text Layout: April Hopkins | aprilhopkins.com

Cartography: Francesca Baerald | francescabaerald.com

ISBN: 9798988140115 (paperback), 9798988140122 (ebook)

To the Reader: War of the Hounds is based on William Shakespeare's Henry V. Certain aspects of this story depart from the stage play while some lines are a clear nod to the original work. I extend all credit and gratitude to the Bard.

To my mom and dad,
it's a brave thing to encourage a strange child.

A STEADY JOURNEY
AND A CLEAR PATH

If you enjoy this novel, **tell others.** Leave a review. Post and share. Corporate publishers have massive marketing budgets—but to keep our airship flying, Seven Coins Media depends on the enthusiasm of people who love fantasy literature. And we wouldn't have it any other way.

Join our Discord community to talk about this book: discord.gg/uney7VT

Note: This book contains monsters. Scan the QR code if you'd like a detailed list of content warnings (possible spoilers).

AMON
Northeast Region
Ringaré Sea
Mahynlleth
Llambé Oromor
Winterhaven
Drymill
Fel Harbor
Silva
Brayford
Guldur
Ebernok
Eloe Vale
Hollywell
Coelan
Barcombe
House Varga
Asher
Whitewood
Star's Path
Laew
Taruithorn
Mountain Keep
Vere
Il Strig
Il Strig Deep
Elm
Ferndale
Overlook
Aylebridge
Maynor Settlemer
Klein
Mountain Palace
of Lord Vaugner
Welton
Danyn
Covenant
The Boundless
Ruins
Ryvenmoor
Senacht
Qualheim
The Kal'tari
Tower
Rengwé
Elud
Qual's Way Station
Atwe

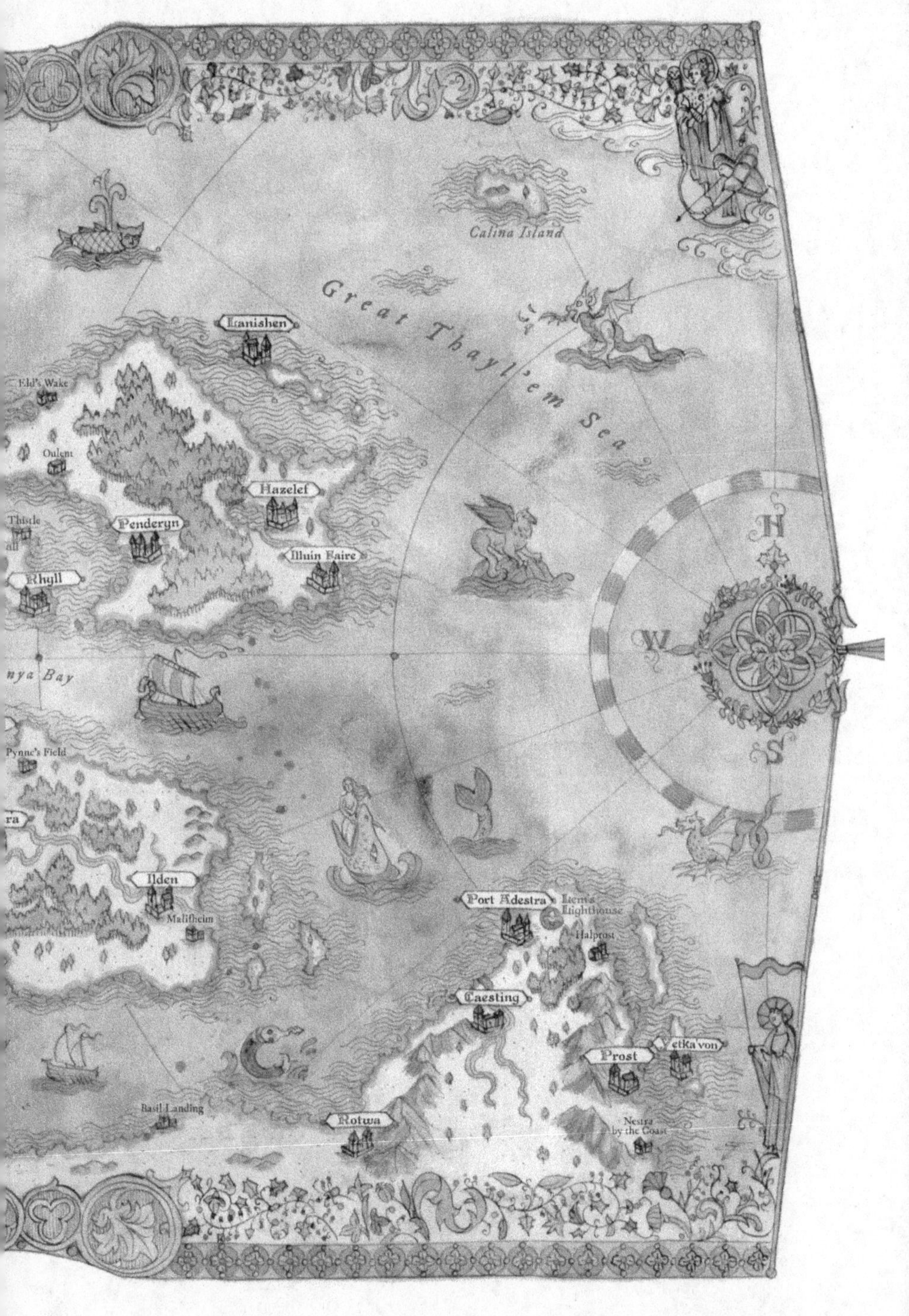

Calina Island
Great Thayl'em Sea
Eld's Wake
Oulent
Thistle Hall
Penderyn
Rhyll
nya Bay
Pynne's Field
ra
Ilden
Malisheim
Basil Landing
Lranishen
Hazelef
Illuin Faire
Rotwa
Port Adestra
Liem's Lighthouse
Halprost
Caesting
Prost
Yetka von
Nesira by the Coast
N
W
S

"But now already all the flocks and herds had been eaten. Nothing remained to fill the insatiable maw of the dragon but the little people of the homes and hearths of all the town. Every day, two children were now given him."

— from St. George and the Dragon, an English fairy tale

I

THE AUDIENCE GATHERED. They sat on the soft, green lawn, waiting for the performance to begin. They chattered among themselves, restless with anticipation. Meanwhile, the actors got ready backstage.

The stage itself was nothing more than a quiet patch of swept dirt in the courtyard. A red curtain hung from a rope, which the actors had stretched across the courtyard earlier that day. They had tied one end of the rope to the balcony of the patron's estate. The other end was tied to a thick tree branch that reached halfway across the courtyard. The tree provided good shade for the villagers who were invited to see the performance.

Hidden behind the red curtain was a bustling, murmuring assemblage of players.

The backstage occupied an open area of the lawn near ivy-covered walls. Wagons positioned along the wall stored the troupe's supplies. Four draft horses grazed at a hay trough nearby. Trunks for costumes and props became the benches actors sat upon while applying their makeup. A few actors got dressed in front of each other. They took their time changing. It was an indolence bordering on exhibitionism.

The veteran actors were in a pleasant mood, joking with one another and gossiping in hushed tones about today's patron and his family. The younger actors paced, practicing lines and going over their vocal exercises. An actor bit the knuckle of her thumb while attempting tongue twisters, "Sweet birds sing songs sweetly while the cat quietly cries." A man on stilts and dressed like a wolf hummed and trilled. A woman dressed as a general walked by—in the opposite direction—reciting a nonsense mantra, "taw-tay-tee-tay, saw-say-see-say, raw-ray-ree-ray." But the youngest among them, Ekor, stood at the edge of the curtain. He wore a mangy, ill-fitted squirrel costume. And despite the old theatre superstition, he looked around the curtain to spy on the audience.

A poet, dressed in a puffy velvet blouse with a ridiculous ruff collar, walked to the center of the stage. He recited a bawdy ballad about two lovers who met in the forest. Ekor didn't think the ballad was any good, too many lines about their breathing and kissing. Everything was heaving and gasping. One second the maiden was forgetting to breathe, and then she was remembering she had forgotten. Deep, excessive exhalations. All too silly. Ekor wondered if courtly love was just a matter of hyperventilating and fainting in each other's embrace.

The audience didn't look impressed either. The people sitting on the ground picked at blades of grass. Their attention wandered to the limbs of the oak tree above them, the branches lazily waving in the breeze, urging them to sneak off.

The troupe had met this wandering poet on their way to perform at the Aylebridge Festival. All the Aylebridge spots were booked, so they relocated to a nearby village. The poet joined them when their previous poet left for another group traveling closer to his hometown.

"Ekor!" the boy's father hissed. "Get back here. You'll curse the performance if anyone sees you before the play begins."

"The damn poet is prattling away!" Ekor hollered. "He's boring the crowd. He'll curse the performance before we ever get the opportunity."

Everyone backstage snickered. Pike, the leader of the troupe, adjusted her wig before turning to respond.

"Be thankful that poet isn't like the one in Illuin Faire. She was gifted by Hebron, a lark, a bard like no other."

"What's wrong with that?"

"We were amateurs by comparison! Everyone was in tears, clapping wildly at whatever verses she threw at them. When we came out, we looked like bumblers. There was no love left for us."

Ekor took a last look at the long-winded poet and then let the curtain go. He saw the stern landowner, their patron, standing at the back, arms folded. This man had given the villagers the day off from working the fields. The villagers arrived hours before the actors were even finished setting up the stage. The villagers brought baskets filled with bread, cheese, dried meats, and wine, and set up picnics throughout the courtyard. They brought their lutes, flutes, and bodhrán drums. Some juggled and others performed acrobatic feats. They entertained themselves while waiting to be entertained. A troupe could find new recruits among the villagers.

The patron wasn't being generous by offering the courtyard outside his home. In a sense, he was held hostage by tradition. A troupe needed a place to perform. They sought the wealthiest family in the region, and the actors refused to perform unless the whole village was invited. It was a financial decision. More people, more coin. The troupe would rather have a chest of silver than a handful of gold. The wealthy family played the reluctant host, while the villagers attracted the actors. And the actors better be worth the trouble because a bad reputation spread faster than they could travel in their horse-drawn wagons.

Pike allowed their host to choose the performance for that afternoon. He wanted to see the *War of the Hounds*, a popular request and a mainstay of any troupe's repertoire.

Even though the terrible war had ended over thirty years ago, a whole generation had grown up with fearful memories of Kret Bonebreaker and his legion. Amon had always dealt with gnolls, ogres, trolls, goblins, and other monstrous creatures. But never had the creatures united under one warlord. People had lost their parents, their siblings. They were displaced and destitute. To this day, the people of Amon clung to the story of a brave Bren Caius who fought for them and emerged victorious. The play, in its many variations, reminded the people of what they had lost and how they survived. Revisiting the war felt like a small violence to heal a greater one.

The poet finished the ballad, suddenly, jarringly—leaving too much open for interpretation. He took a curt bow. The villagers offered scattered applause, confused, wondering if this was how the poem went. The poet, instead of retreating behind the curtain, marched through the crowd and off into the fields. Where he was going, no one knew.

"Dammit, Ekor," Pike said. "The poet must've heard you."

Pike grabbed her velveteen coat and waved at the other actors.

"Get ready! I'll stall the crowd for a bit."

Ekor had been ready for a while. His dad had dressed him in the squirrel outfit before tending to his own makeup and costume. Ekor was old enough to put the costume on by himself, but his dad wanted to do it. His dad was also fussy about where the costumes were stowed and how they were folded. Everyone did it the wrong way, except his dad. He insisted that doing it the right way was the only way they had room for everything else.

Ekor hated the squirrel outfit. It fit him two years ago, but he had grown since then—and he seemed to be the only person to realize it. The outfit sleeves and pant legs were too short. It chafed in unmentionable places. Worst of all, it smelled. Musty, stale, and with a peculiar ripeness. The stench lived within the matted fur of the costume that was once soft and fluffy. No amount of washing could remove the smell. The smell only got worse. Ekor had complained to Pike, but she did not consider replacing the costume as an option. She had worn it when she was young—for a different performance—and now it was Ekor's turn to be the squirrel. His only comfort was knowing one day he could bequeath the costume to his younger sister.

Pike adjusted the sleeves of her coat. And then she stepped onto the stage. The crowd went silent with anticipation. Pike had this effect on people, an overwhelming presence. It made her ideal as the chorus. Without saying a word, she had their attention. The distracted audience put down the plucked blades of grass and dandelions. They ceased their conversations and looked up. Pike opened her mouth to speak and then paused. She held up a finger, gesturing for them to give her a moment. She leaned in to speak again, and again paused, and then a third time. The audience laughed. Before their laughter died down, she began her monologue.

"May the muses within the walls of our honorable patron's house grow curious about this preceding. May they drift this way and inspire our work. Muses come!" Pike shouted these last words and waited for a response. Once contented, she continued. "Here's your part: Imagine for a moment that the humble swept stage is a battlefield. The actors are generals, soldiers, hounds, and other assorted characters both familiar and unfamiliar to you. Do this, and I promise the scenes will extend beyond this earthy circle and take new shape in an open mind."

Pike began most performances with these words or some variation. This prologue was essential—no one wanted to start the play with an audience that wasn't ready. The prologue existed to warm the crowd and prepare them for something wondrous. Even the grumpy patron uncrossed his arms and appeared to soften at Pike's opening.

"In a moment, you will see the warlike Bren Caius enter, the young high general who led her small army against Kret Bonebreaker and his legion. She will appear much like Olar, the god of death, with the dogs of war driven before her. But this stage is not worthy of the true Bren Caius. She is too great. So, forgive us for this replacement, this counterfeit." On cue, the actor playing Bren looked out from behind the curtain and scowled. More laughter. Pike continued. "Can this stage represent that final battle at Pynne's Field when Bren the Beloved and Kret Bonebreaker, a fearsome gnoll more powerful than any other, faced each other in single combat, all for the fate of Amon? Can this stage hold every soldier who gave their life to so worthy a cause? No, we must take this small space and magnify it. We can do so if your imagination allows. Will you join us?"

Pike saw a few people nod in agreement, and she had them. "I admire your enthusiasm, but you are not ready for Pynne's Field and the great drama that will unfold there. We must retreat a few days before—farther to the east, near Ilden, where the tulips were trampled by these opposing fronts, led by those two mighty generals, the cruel Kret and Bren herself." Pike held out her hands, melodramatically begging for forgiveness. "Don't dwell too much on our imperfections. It's not a competition. We actors are here because we love what we do, and we'd do it for free, if we were able to feast on your applause." This was absolutely untrue, but Pike said it anyway. Coin could buy many more pleasures than just their next meal. The actors were great admirers of being well paid. So no one could steal their coin, they even had an arcane crate, which they purchased from a mage in Thistle. The coin mattered. "Let's keep it simple. When we talk of horses, you should see them stamping their proud hooves upon the earth. Your thoughts will decorate our high general and carry her across Amon." Pike leaned near a boy sitting at the front. Pike put her hand to the side of her mouth as if speaking only to the boy. "And let's hope the outcome of this play mirrors our history. I couldn't handle the tears if we should lose today!" A one-armed man near the back of the crowd, old enough to be a veteran, hooted loudly. A person nearby patted him on the shoulder. "While the War of the Hounds took place over several years, we shall abbreviate it. Two turns of an hourglass? We can drag it out to three or four if you want. What say you?" The crowd groaned. Some shouted down the suggestion. "Fine then. Fine. Two hours. I will be your chorus to this history. Be patient with me. But who approaches? Let's listen and see."

Three actors walked onto the stage. They each wore a strip of fur across their shoulders, a rudimentary gnoll costume. The actors hissed and growled and snapped at the audience, who welcomed them with lively booing.

This moment was a cathartic one, and Pike always gave it plenty of time.

Wherever they traveled, the actors heard stories of loved ones killed by gnolls. People needed an opportunity to face their tormentors, to reduce them to waddling characters on a stage, and to believe such monsters could be slain.

* * *

The tulips were planted in rows by color. The rows were spaced with enough room between each row for a worker to walk down the line and harvest the tulips. Each row was about an arm's length, so the workers could reach easily across to gather the tulips. There were two rows of red, two rows of yellow, two rows of purple, then orange, pink, and white. The pattern repeated down the field.

The tulip blossoms bobbed in the breeze. Each one moving back and forth. The farmers of Ilden said when the tulips danced, it was time to harvest.

Harvest time had come.

The gnolls trekked across the tulips, cutting diagonal lines through the field. The gnolls were human-like beasts with heads like hyenas, blood-matted fur underneath the scrap leather armor, each one carrying whatever shield they salvaged from the fallen, holding an axe or sword or spear. One gnoll pulled a tulip, bulb and all, and tucked it underneath his pauldron as decoration. The tulip hung limply, bouncing with the gnoll's every step.

The gnolls were spaced far apart, not unlike the tulip rows, as the archers from the Northern Army fired volley after volley. Most gnolls held their shields high to receive the attack, while others fell into the flowers, a final yelp before dying. But even as their numbers decreased, they marched forward.

The gnolls were closing in on the archers and would soon charge.

The line of fearful archers looked to their sergeant, Leylan, waiting for her order to retreat, but she did not give the command.

Bren Caius and her calvary had been pulled away to another part of the battle, leaving the archers behind. As high general, she was tasked with the impossible role of being everywhere on the battlefield, protecting everyone, and leading them all to victory, happiness, and prosperity. Bren had assured them she would return, but she was nowhere to be seen.

"Another!" Leylan shouted. Her face was grim. Her upper lip twitched in anger. She hated this war, but she hated the gnolls more. Each archer pulled an arrow from the quiver. "Nock!" The archers fitted their arrows on the bow strings. "Draw and loose!"

An archer's draw arm spasmed from the exertion of repeatedly firing. It had been a long day, but the battle was not over. The archer tried, but he could only pull the bow halfway. When the arrow was loosed, it didn't even make it to the line of gnolls. The archers had weakened the encroaching gnoll lines, but not enough.

"Soldiers, drop your bows," Leylan reached for the hilt of her sword. "Draw your swords."

Her troops panicked, all of them crumpling in half from the command as dry leaves cast onto the fire. They folded with wild gestures of dismay and crackled with protests. "But ma'am," sputtered Haim, the next in command, "we're archers! We're not foot soldiers."

Haim was the last and late-born child of a large family. He was adored and doted on, but not much was expected of him. A well-meaning boy in need of a trade and a sensible direction in life. He had joined the war when three of his siblings had been killed. Haim wanted to avenge his family, but he also wanted to make a name for himself. Since that day, he became acquainted with how little courage he had. Haim regretted his decision to become a soldier with every long march, every poor night's sleep, and every terrifying encounter with the hounds.

"Are those swords decorative?" Leylan loudly berated Haim. "Did Bren give them to the wrong people?" He was not sure how to respond. Leylan shouted again, inches from his face. "Draw—your—sword!"

The men and women fumbled for their weapons. Leylan fixed her eyes upon the gnolls. She had been waiting for this moment. Leylan raised her sword and ran ahead of her soldiers. "Charge!"

The soldiers did not follow their sergeant. They searched for some courage among them, but there was none to be found. The swords dangled in their hands, useless.

Leylan had shared stories with Haim about how her father had served in the Northern Army under High General Gwaine Abar, who preceded Marcus Tom. Leylan's father returned to his family with honors and wreaths celebrating his valor.

Leylan said she wanted to be like her father. She wanted the wreath.

Leylan turned around to see that she alone had rushed toward the gnolls. Leylan locked eyes with Haim, and Haim saw the sober realization on her face that she would die. Valor mattered little if the people by your side were cowards. She had no choice but to hold her shield and swing her sword. Perhaps she could kill a few more.

The gnolls swarmed Leylan, stabbing and slashing at her with spear and sword and axe. She fought back, but all strength had drained from her. Her strikes lacked force.

Haim heard Leylan scream with each rending blow. It was the worst sound he had ever heard, and it rang out across the field. Lifeless, still and drenched in her own blood, Leylan fell to the ground among the tulips.

Haim just stood and watched.

In that moment, a barn owl soared above, a white herald against white clouds. Bren's owl, Ruth, went ahead of the high general in every battle.

Bren Caius hadn't abandoned them.

War horses thundered across the tulip rows—first red, then yellow, purple, orange, pink, and then white. The cavalry tore through the gnoll infantry. The gnolls not trampled by the horses were run through with steel-tipped lances. After the initial charge, the riders dropped their lances and drew their swords. With a synchronized pull of the reins, they turned their horses about and galloped back toward the scattered gnolls.

Bren rode with the calvary. She wore gleaming plate armor. It had a golden sheen when the sunlight hit it. She might have blended in with the other soldiers except the armor shined so brightly. She did not wear a visor to cover her face. Instead, she wore a chainmail coif with a kettle helmet. She chose the kettle helmet over the visor to improve her range of sight. Bren looked from side to side, shouting orders to the other soldiers. More important than her sword was her complete understanding of the battlefield. Where were the weak points in the formation, and where was the opposition strongest? Had any of her soldiers fallen and did they need a hand up? As general, she became her soldiers' eyes, and they trusted her vision.

Bren's owl circled overhead, signaling to troops farther away where the locus of the battle was.

The gnolls converged on Bren Caius. One gnoll jumped up and grabbed the back of her breastplate, pulling her off her mount. Rather than fighting against the weight of the gnoll, she rolled with it, backward and landing on her feet, executed so perfectly it appeared as though she did it on purpose. The poets—who had never seen her in battle—liked to describe Bren's fighting style as graceful, acrobatic, or like a dance, but the best word to describe Bren with a sword was "efficient." No movement was wasted. No needless flourishes. One motion, one strike, one kill, and then she would move to the next gnoll. Bren understood endurance was crucial. Anything that might waste her energy could cost her later in the fight. She needed to maintain her strength and her stamina. Any showy spins or whirlwind attacks were a dangerous vanity. To the unschooled, Bren's fighting style was boring, but to the experienced warrior, her approach was a masterclass in melee combat, an inspiration to champion fighters.

Bren saw the weak point, the unprotected chink, and she drove her sword into it.

Bren noticed a soldier guarding his left side, and she would strike at his right side.

Bren would find the one gnoll who wasn't paying attention, and she would attack him before he even saw it coming.

In this way, she dominated on the field. It had little to do with prowess or strength, though she had both. She observed, and she took advantage of every opportunity. Each move was the correct one.

The archers under Leylan's command watched Bren's calvary thin the enemy down to nothing. They saw Bren Caius, like a god of war, slaughter the gnolls, and it emboldened them. Too late for Leylan, but Haim and the other soldiers finally raised their swords and charged in, as victory was a forgone conclusion.

* * *

The evening after a battle was not a time for celebration. Quiet enveloped everyone. Each soldier found a place at one of the campfires to sit and to think on what they had witnessed. Memories only a few hours old were a blur—a confusion of erratic shouts and commands. Nothing made sense. They realized survival was not a matter of skill or cleverness, but dumb luck. As firelight glowed on empty faces, each soldier understood there was no reason for one person to live and for another to fall. A soldier could drown such thoughts in drink, but ale and mead were for the return home, that and the feast a grateful family would prepare. Instead, the soldier had tepid water, hard bread, and thoughts of loved ones who could never understand what happened during the war.

Talking about home was not something that was done by the veterans. And at this point in the war, only veterans remained. The neophytes wouldn't shut up about life back home and what their plans were for when they returned. They sang songs around the campfire and made friends quickly. They were the first ones to die on the battlefield. Fate was fickle and a great lover of irony. The veteran knew to not tempt such misfortune with foolish words. Instead, follow orders, trust Bren Caius, eat and rest when possible, fight the hounds, and someday go home. For those who would return home, they carried this silence of the evening after a battle with them. At a time when they should unburden their pain, they held to it more closely until it became a weight around their necks. Their shoulders slumped, and they could no longer look up. They no longer knew how to let go of the thing that almost killed them.

On the evening after the Ilden battle, the soldiers were lost in contemplation.

Haim sat alone in the dark and cried. His hands covered his face. He was ashamed. Well aware Bren had saved him from a cowardly death.

"Tomorrow morning, we'll execute the archers. Every last one of them."

Bren ranted as she paced the large tent, avoiding the many low-hanging, multi-colored lanterns. Aubec Skarsol and Oren of Angnavir watched her. They were her advisors, war mage and battle-hardened swordmaster, respectively. Both offered a unique perspective on their deadly business.

Oren was a brutish warrior from Raustfweg. A bear of a man, broad and muscular. Everything about his presence was a threat. He had the dull expression of a beast in his territory. No smaller creature would dare approach. Like many from Raust-fweg, the braiding in Oren's long beard and the tattoos on his face all told a story. To someone who could read the braids and inked runes, they'd know he was in Amon because he had killed a family member long ago and was an outcast from his home village. Wherever he died, there he would be buried. There would be no return home, even in death. And so, he lived as a person who was already dead and did not fear what had already come.

While Oren exuded predatory dominance, Aubec was the picture of sophistication. Aubec was a rakish mage, beautiful and genteel. His father came from a noble Aylebridge family. His mother lauded as a masterful alchemist. Aubec followed the family tradition of greatness, earning his renown as a scholar hungry for life and all its mysteries.

Whereas Oren was fair skinned with an icy complexion, Aubec's dark skin had a warmth to it. Oren's eyes threatened violence; Aubec's eyes were kind and reassuring. Oren shaved his head and let his beard grow; the thick strands of Aubec's hair revealed a meticulous pride in his appearance, along with his clean-shaven face. Oren dressed for battle in brown leather and wool; Aubec's vibrant red cape was an unnecessary vanity, which made him stand out among the masses.

Despite their differences, Oren and Aubec both knew better than to interrupt Bren during one of her many drunken tantrums.

"Every last one of them!" Bren had wild, bloodshot eyes. "We line them up in front of everyone, and we slit their cowardly throats one after another. Then, we send a letter to each of their families and let them know how shamefully they acted on the field. An embarrassment." She addressed no one but herself. "May hell be emptied of its devils, for they're all here. Some days, I would prefer to lead Kret's army into battle.

At least, then, I wouldn't have to stand side by side with cowards. Is there anything worse than a coward, a worthless man who values himself above everyone else? Let's execute the archers. Let it serve as a lesson to the others."

Bren turned to Aubec and Oren, daring a response. Aubec swirled his wine around and tried his best to not sound like he was challenging his general. He spoke casually, as if these ideas were coming to him on a whim.

"What's the lesson? We're low on archers. We need them. They're one of the few advantages we have over the gnolls. The gnolls are piss poor with bows, and we're not."

"We can't win a war," Bren grumbled, "with soldiers who won't follow orders."

"They're archers. With only three orders to follow." Aubec held up three fingers to count them. "Nock, draw, and loose." Aubec waved his three fingers back and forth, a common crude gesture in Amon. Bren's rage abated as she smiled at Aubec's humor.

"You're wrong," Oren spoke in a low, threatening growl. Everything he said sounded like a threat. "They're not archers. They're soldiers. And there's only *one* order they should follow. Which is?"

Oren waited for Aubec to respond. Aubec conceded the point.

"Whatever their commanding officer tells them."

"Whatever their commanding officer tells them." Oren cracked his knuckles, pressing his palm against his closed fist. "If Leylan says run at the hounds with nothing but a willow branch and a bag of horse manure, they better do it."

"There's an image," Aubec said. "I hear what you're saying, but these are rational, fearful humans we have to command.

They're not going to run to their death. This isn't Raustfweg. Olar isn't going to reward them for dying in battle."

"Even in Raustfweg, soldiers fear death. But we give our lives for something greater than ourselves. If we don't trust our leaders, we still die, but we do it in vain."

"You give the leaders too much credit," Bren said. "Sometimes, a wasted life is a wasted life. We can't redeem them with sound battle tactics. Aubec is right," she looked at Aubec, "but don't let it go to your head."

"I never do." Aubec nodded cordially.

"Charging the hounds was suicide wrapped in valor. You're right. But I'm sorry, Aubec. Oren is right in the way that matters."

"Excuse me?" Aubec asked.

"In that I agree with Oren. We can't have soldiers disobeying an order, any order. We're on the verge of winning this war, losing this war, or outright mutiny. It's all possible. Fate is dancing on the edge of a sword's blade, and the slightest misstep will cost us everything. Cowardice guides their hearts. If our soldiers must live in fear, let them be more afraid of disappointing me than of dying on the battlefield."

"You've had too much to drink." Aubec said these words under his breath before clearing his throat and speaking louder. "My general, my northern light, if we execute the archers for their cowardice, we won't have any more archers. Hm?"

"If these archers are so useful, why do they need us to save them?" Bren's face twisted in anger. Her eyes were red from drink and rage.

Aubec knew he couldn't push too much. "Each part of our army depends on the other. Separate us and our weaknesses become more obvious."

"It's not *our* army. It's mine. Never forget."

"Yes, Bren." Aubec took a long drink and finished his wine. "But do not forget, I serve the people of Amon, not you."

"You're rather bold tonight."

Aubec laughed. "I'm quite the opposite, general. I speak because I fear further failure. Nothing more." Aubec pulled the locs of his hair back and tied them with a red sash.

"Speak your mind, mage."

"The trees."

"The trees?" Bren was genuinely confused by his response.

"When we approached this warband, I saw cleared trees beyond the tulip fields. The gnolls' camp had axes and other lumbering tools. Everywhere we find the gnolls, they're cutting down trees."

"Are they gathering timber for siege weapons, for ship building?"

"That's the odd thing. The felled trees remain. They aren't collecting the lumber. They cut down the trees just to cut them down. It makes no sense."

Bren's head was too foggy from the wine. She was in no mood to ponder the erratic behavior of gnolls.

"Leave me, both of you. I need to think. I will see you again in the morning."

Aubec and Oren both stood up, bowed, and left the tent.

Bren was alone. For the first time in several days, she was alone. The recent campaign had forced them to march across the lower peninsula, along the southern coast of Tu'enya Bay, chasing after smaller fragments of Kret's scattered army. When possible, they would fight the easy battles. If they outnumbered a warband, they struck hard. But if the odds were in question, they would pick at them with a series of skirmishes and retreats. It carved away at Kret's remaining force, but it also exhausted Bren's army to the point of delirium. And Kret Bonebreaker was nowhere to be found.

Before the war, no one had heard of Kret Bonebreaker or where he had come from. Rumors spread of how a gnoll—twice as large and infinitely more ruthless than a typical gnoll—rallied all the creatures that lurked in nighttime stories and in the imaginations of disquieted children, the creatures that hid in the dark places, in strange forests, underneath bridges and beds. It took a long time before the rumors were confirmed because Kret left no survivors. He wiped entire villages off the map. His march across Amon was well underway while Bren was still struggling to assemble the small army her predecessor, Marcus Tom, had left her.

Today's fight should have never happened. Bren had been using Kret's strategy of attrition against him, and he responded by sending his troops far and wide. For every warband they found, there were five others left to raid across the countryside. Bren's scouting had been their primary advantage. Now it meant little. She didn't need to chase warbands. She needed to find Kret, to cut off the head, but he had disappeared. Meanwhile, Bren's army was beginning to question her at every turn. Any time they were confronted with a setback or disappointment, they whined to Bren, wondering how the world could be so cruel. They didn't always do it with their words, but she could see the defeat in their eyes. In their pitiful silence, they pleaded to return to their farms and their families. Only Aubec and Oren would challenge her, and even they were beginning to weaken. Aubec would no longer push back like he had at the beginning of the war, and Oren seemed all too eager to die on the field.

Bren wandered the tent, lost in her thoughts. Her mind could not leave the battlefield. She was always there. Always fighting, her sword in one hand, her shield in the other, and Kret was always across from her. But no matter how close she got, he was out of reach. In this way, he taunted her.

No one could match her in battle, except Kret. He would be formidable. He was stronger, faster, and much smarter than a typical dog-brained gnoll. She would fight him, if she could find him, and she would end this war.

Bren grabbed a cup of wine and, realizing it was empty, she threw it across the tent. It clattered against her plate armor, which hung on a wooden stand. The stand tottered, while the armor clanged against the wooden post.

As though the cacophony of cup against armor was a summoning bell, Yulie the cupbearer arrived obediently with another flagon of wine. Yulie was young, still a child. Her curly red hair bobbed as she moved about. Freckles covered her round face.

"More wine, princess?"

If anyone else had called Bren by a noble honorific, she would have struck them where they stood. Bren wasn't fighting this war to grab more power for herself. But "prince" and "princess" were common terms of endearment for the folk of Ebernok, where Yulie's family came from. Bren allowed it. The one person you didn't want to upset was the person bringing you wine.

"Yes, please. Thank you, Yulie."

Bren was about to pick up her cup from the ground, but Yulie had already rushed to retrieve it. Yulie poured a full glass and handed it to Bren Caius. When Bren took the cup, Yulie curtsied.

"Yulie?"

"Yes, princess."

"Before you retire for the evening, can you tell me a story? One from Ebernok, perhaps. I need something to quiet my mind. The wine isn't enough."

Yulie was not one given to banter. She was quiet and did not yield to Bren's gregarious nature. Maybe she was always this way, or maybe she was once a giggling, playful little girl and tragedy stripped her of that liveliness. Bren would never know. Yulie's family had been slaughtered by the gnolls a few months ago, which placed her in Bren's care and service. Yulie did not say much; she did her job, and she served well. And whenever the high general asked for a story, Yulie told a story.

Yulie spoke quietly, gently. She recited the story as though the words might vanish if she didn't handle them with care.

"One day unlike any other, a dragon emerged from their long slumber, and they were hungry. The dragon was named Vorghenmauller. The nearby village was afraid of the dragon, and they offered the dragon their livestock to eat. But after a short while, Vorghenmauller had eaten all the sheep, all the pigs, and all the cattle and chickens. The villagers had nothing left for themselves except gruel and leeks. With no more livestock for the dragon, they offered Vorghenmauller the children from the village. The villagers would cast lots to see which child was next."

Bren Caius had heard this story before. She was born in Eloe Vale. More accurately, she was swaddled and left on a doorstep in Eloe Vale. But the family that claimed her had originally lived farther to the west, nearer Ebernok, where the story of Vorghenmauller was common. The version Yulie told was the one most familiar to Bren. She always wondered why the villagers went from livestock to children. Why wouldn't the parents sacrifice themselves? Why wouldn't they fight back?

Bren finished her wine in a long, greedy gulp and held it out for Yulie to refill. Yulie filled the cup and continued the story.

"As fate would have it, the king's own daughter was to be sacrificed. The great king loved his daughter very much, and his heart broke at the thought of giving her over to Vorghenmauller."

"And the villagers didn't love their children?" Bren drunkenly scoffed. "The king wasn't so great."

"Excuse me, princess?"

"Nothing, continue."

"First, the king went to the most honorable knight. He asked him, 'Will you fight the dragon and save my daughter?' But the knight knew it would be certain death. He had to refuse the king because if he died, who would continue his charitable work? Surely, saving one princess wasn't more important than a lifetime of good deeds, which he had planned. The king was disappointed, but he went to a second knight, the wisest knight in the land. The king asked him, 'Will you fight the dragon and save my daughter?' But this knight knew that if he killed this dragon, it would only enrage other dragons, and they would come to this land seeking revenge. He had to refuse the king because surely one dragon was better than a hundred. Finally, the king went to his bravest knight and asked him to slay the dragon. The king had offered the knight riches, but the knight refused it all. The knight merely wanted to fulfill his obligation to the king and slay the cruel Vorghenmauller. He bowed and said, 'King, I am yours to command.' And he set off to find the dragon."

There was more to the story, how the knight was clever, studying Vorghenmauller from a distance and learning his weakness. But Bren did not hear the rest of the story. Bren had collapsed on her cot, asleep with a head full of dragons and a belly full of wine and devoured children.

* * *

Bren jolted awake. She heard a commotion outside the tent. She reached for her sword, usually sheathed and lying next to her, but it was not there. The sword was on the floor on the other side of the tent. Bren tried to stand up. Her balance was unsteady, and her head ached from last night's wine. A throbbing, queasy feeling pressed her on all sides.

"The named gods. Never again." Bren gave her false oath, a common morning ritual. "I'm never drinking that much wine. Never again."

Oren walked into the tent. Sunlight exploded behind him, and it pained Bren to look in that direction. Kret Bonebreaker might have been her greatest enemy, but the morning had been her most enduring foe.

Bren saw Oren's dour countenance. No attack was taking place; Oren smiled whenever a fight was imminent. He couldn't help it.

"*Sah'le vuk!* Oren! What's going on in the camp?"

"Kret's emissary has arrived. Speck, that nasty goblin mage, has entered our camp and requests an audience."

"Speck? Here?" Bren walked behind a paneled screen as she yanked her nightgown over her head. She changed into her formal attire, an embroidered doublet with a short cape that hung over one shoulder and wide-legged pants gathered at the ankles. She then pulled on her black leather boots. She stepped out and presented herself to Oren. "How do I look?"

"You're wearing courtly clothes," Oren said, unimpressed. "But you still look like you slept in a ditch." Oren pointed at her hair. "You have some dried blood—"

She swatted his hand away. "If Speck wanted a kinder version of me, he should've come later in the day."

Bren stepped out of the tent, adjusting the sleeves of her doublet. She glared at the sun as the sun glared back at her. Speck waited nearby—a grotesque goblin, hunched over, boils and warts upon his bare back. He was surrounded by wary soldiers with spears and swords pointed at him. No one was taking a chance on this mage. Speck looked up at Bren with his white milky eyes and smiled, jagged teeth from end to end.

"Good morning, Bren Caius. I come here on behalf of Kret Bonebreaker with a message and a gift." He held the gift, wrapped in parchment, swaddled like a baby. Bren eyed the gift warily.

"Give me the message first."

"Aren't you going to show the basic customs of hospitality? I am, after all, a guest. I haven't even been offered tea."

"We're at war. You're not a stranger. Unless you come with Kret's head wrapped in that parchment, I have no hospitality to offer."

Bren heard a commotion farther back in the camp. She instinctively shifted her sight to the closest animal, which, in this instance, was a horse tethered to a post.

All her life, Bren had a supernatural ability to perceive through the senses of nearby animals. She did not understand this power, nor did many people know about it. She used it as a child to scout and satisfy her curiosity. As she grew older, her powers increased. She could control these animals with simple commands, urging them to go one way or another.

Through the horse's eyes, with its wider visual field and limited color spectrum, she saw Aubec running to join Bren and the group gathered outside her tent. She wasn't the only one who had been asleep when Speck arrived. As the Northern Army's sole mage, Aubec's presence was needed. Bren shifted her sight back to herself just as Aubec nudged his way through the crowd.

"Dammit. Let me through," Aubec muttered. "Bren, terribly sorry."

"Aubec, my old friend," Speck said dryly. "I'm so glad you're here to protect the high general from the dark and twisted goblin mage. We can all breathe a sigh of relief."

Aubec ignored Speck's prodding and instead looked to Bren for acknowledgement and forgiveness. Bren gave both with a nod.

"If this were an assassination attempt, I believe Speck's best opportunity has passed," Bren reasoned. "He wouldn't dare try now. He really is here on a diplomatic errand."

Bren motioned for her guards to open the tent flaps.

"Come, shadows and friends. Follow me into the tent."

Yulie poured tea for Bren and her guests. This special blend helped ease headaches after a night of drinking. Bren gratefully accepted the tea with both hands and took a long gulp from it. After setting down her cup, Bren acknowledged Speck.

"Did you want greater fanfare?" Bren spoke in a mocking tone. "'Oh look, it's Speck, the venerable war mage of Kret Bonebreaker.' No, I do not esteem you. You're demon-spawn, a worthless heap of flesh, a hideous foul nothing. Say what you came here to say, then leave."

Speck pushed the tea away. "I was hoping for a little civility."

"You'll get none from me."

"I gathered as much."

"What treasure does Kret have for me, goblin? What message?"

Speck took the wrapped gift and unrolled it. He placed it at Bren's feet. A bouquet of tulips, all the colors from the fields of Ilden.

"The gift *is* the message," Speck said. "No clever or mocking words. No requests or demands. The war continues."

"Kret wanted to give me flowers? That's the message?"

"As far as I can gather, yes."

Bren looked at the flowers for a long time. She prodded them with the toe of her boot.

"Kret has murdered untold scores of my kinfolk. He has burned fields and left farmers without their crops, starving us before we could ever meet him on the field of battle. For these several months, we've searched for your army—only to find small warbands to pick apart and tear down. You have eluded us. You have confounded us. And now, Kret brings flowers?" Bren's voice rose in pitch as she asked this question, cracking in her frenzy. "I can guess at the meaning. Is he saying Bren should stop fighting and bear children? Expectant parents offer flowers to the named goddess Yoon, the Great Midwife, in hopes of a safe delivery. Just as the flowering plant bears fruit, so does the reddened flowering womb. It's also the mark of adoption, the commitment to raise a child. Or perhaps Kret thinks of me as his daughter. The war has endeared me to him.

I have won favor with savagery to match his own. Am I to visit him on the feasting holidays?" Bren struggled to find words to express her anger and weariness. Bren kicked the flowers, scattering them. She screamed. "I don't care! I want to know where he is! I want to face him in single combat. And I want to be done with this damn war. Him. Me. No emissaries. No war bands. Let's fight it out like two wronged patrons in a tavern. One of us gets dragged out, and the other can finish their drink and live out their short, cursed life."

"A third interpretation." Speck dared to speak. "Perhaps Kret believes the victor of this war will give birth to a new nation?"

"Leave!" Bren shouted at him. She fumbled for her sword on the ground. By the time she had it drawn and was ready to strike at the goblin, he had blinked away.

Aubec smirked. "This was a merry message."

"Shush," Bren said. Motes of blue light twinkled around her. Her eyes were closed. She was seeing through the eyes of Ruth. The owl had taken to the sky the moment Speck disappeared. Bren could see all the soldiers in the camp below. The shadow of the owl moved along the ground. Outside the camp, she saw Speck, teleporting from one place to another several yards ahead, and then reappearing again, farther away. In this fashion, Speck escaped the camp, teleporting these short distances in a crooked path, never a straight line, never in a way that could be easily anticipated. Bren didn't know if this was an aspect of the spell or his preference. Either way, Bren had to concentrate with all her might to follow him. Wherever he was headed, it would lead to Kret.

Several hours passed. Speck continued his journey. Ruth followed. Bren had never extended her animal sight this far.

The strain was immense, but she could not give up. Speck's foolish visitation was her chance at finding her enemy and ending the war.

Finally, she saw a mass of creatures, an army marching westward, thousands more gnolls than what they had encountered the day before. And at the front of the march was Kret Bonebreaker, a shadowy figure towering over the rest.

Bren fell to the ground. She was hungry. Her throat was dry. Her head pounded worse than before. Yulie rushed to her side.

"Princess! Are you well? What did you see?"

"Pynne's Field," Bren gasped. "They're marching to Pynne's Field."

*　*　*

The actor playing Bren Caius got off the ground and patted her pant legs to remove the dirt. Ekor's father held a long pole from behind the curtain, which extended over the top. An owl poppet dangled from a rope fastened to the end of the pole. His father walked back and forth to make it look like the owl was flying. Bren walked offstage, and the owl was removed from the scene. The crowd applauded politely.

Pike stepped onto the stage and scowled at the audience, not satisfied with their level of enthusiasm. The audience laughed and applauded again, louder this time.

Backstage, the actors rushed about, getting ready for the next scene. Ekor's squirrel had nothing to do until the beginning of act four, when Bren would use this small creature to spy on the soldiers. Bren's magical second sight had been a secret, but the common folk found out about it after her death.

This sight became the subject of much speculation—and a popular addition to the performance. Ekor stayed busy folding costumes being thrown at him and grabbing new outfits for the actors who were cast in multiple roles. Speck shushed a younger actor, complaining about a missed line in the scene outside the tent. The exchange was supposed to be longer, but Aubec missed his cue and got on stage late. That was partially Ekor's fault. He couldn't find the red cape. While it wasn't necessary for the scene, the prop was important to the actor. He loved to turn and twirl with the cape.

Pike began her monologue.

"All the youth of Bren's army were on fire—not in the literal sense. That comes later." The audience groaned. Pike's masterful delivery sold even the weakest word play. "The soldiers were on fire, enthusiastic to be on the chase again, now that they knew where Kret was. Any silken idleness at the camp was set aside in wardrobe and trunk as they marched to war."

Pike went into the crowd while continuing her speech. The story was familiar to everyone, so the actors knew they had to find ways to surprise the audience—like venturing off the stage. It had little to do with the story itself and more with their craft.

"But not everyone in Amon was for Amon. Excuse me," Pike said as she stumbled through. "I beg your pardon!" Pike playfully swatted at a young man, implying he had intruded on her space. When, in fact, she had intruded on him. "Little did Bren know that Pynne's Field was not Kret's actual destination. The demon intended to continue westward to Gandryll, where six wealthy families schemed to give Kret's army sanctuary and supplies, turning the dishonorable city into a home base."

Pike stepped past a few more folk and then sat down next

to a woman. Pike helped herself to an apple in the woman's picnic basket. Pike took a large bite and then, with a full mouth, continued her monologue. "Three corrupted men enter. One, Lem of the Cain-Oldcastle family, and the second, Henrik of Masham, and the third, Tomas of Umber—O guilty trio—we shall confirm conspiracy with Kret Bonebreaker. Listen, so we may accurately account for their wrongdoing."

Three actors entered, dressed as nobles, each wearing dark red leather gloves. Pike booed, louder than everyone else, and threw her apple at Henrik, who grabbed it and also took a bite.

"The sum is paid!" Pike shouted at the actors. There was such hurt in her voice. All humor drained from her. The crowd quieted. "The traitors are agreed. The scene is now transported, gentles, to Gandryll. There is a stage." Pike said these words with derision. "You see it plainly. And here we sit. From Ilden, we'll take you to Gandryll and bring you back. We'll do it gently. When Bren is ready for us, we'll return to her. But for now, we shift our scene."

* * *

With the back of his gloved hand, Henrik wiped the juice off his chin. Before he had finished chewing, he took another bite of the apple. More juice dribbled down his chin and again he wiped it. He chewed loudly with an open mouth. A person of such high status should be more mannerly. But for Henrik, being a noble meant he could act however he wanted. No one would dare correct his behavior.

The three nobles stood outside the dilapidated tavern near the cockfighting pit. The pit was three feet deep, with a fence along the circumference. The spectators surrounded the pit, leaning forward, eager to watch the next fight. Within the crowd, people exchanged slips of paper to confirm their bets. They showed each other their coin bags, so the other knew the bet would be covered.

"So," Henrik swallowed down the chunks and took another bite. "Do we have any word from our associate, Kret?"

Tomas and Lem looked aghast, surprised Henrik would say the name out loud.

"No one cares." Henrik waved, gesturing to the commoners. No one acknowledged their presence or their words. All attention was on the cockfight about to begin. Henrik tossed his half-eaten apple to the ground.

"Kret—" Tomas said the word, barely a whisper, "—has sent word that his army is traveling with all haste to Gandryll. They need provisions. They need our walls. They need our ships. They need a home base. If we let them in and give over the city, their victory is assured. They can outlast Bren's remnants. It changes everything."

"And the warlord has agreed to our terms? He will spare our families and our allies if we give him sanctuary?" Henrik asked. Tomas and Lem both dutifully nodded. Henrik put his arms around his fellow conspirators and brought them in close. "Focus on the end: Bren Caius dead and her troops scattered. We can rule over the ruins. Kret has no interest in Amon. He wants to burn it down, then he'll migrate elsewhere. Think of him as a swarm of locusts, not a king. We can repair the damage, but not if the war continues. We're saving lives by bringing this madness to a conclusion."

"If Kret wins," Lem spoke while watching over his shoulder, "we profit. If he loses, we say we were the victims. He invaded our city and took over. What could we do?"

Tomas put his hand on Lem's chest to quiet him.

"Don't be so foolish to think you're clever. What we're doing is risky. There's no getting around it. We're giving aid to the enemy, and in a few days, we'll give them the walls of this city and our ships. If we fail, I encourage you to fall on your swords before Bren finds you."

Two ragged men in the pit each held a rooster. They tossed the chickens to the center and then moved back. The chickens' feathers fanned out around their necks, a warning sign to the other. With a flurry of flapping wings and extended talons, the roosters crashed into one another. The crowd shouted. The movements of the birds were a blur as they bounded up and down, trying to get over their rival. The combat was a confusing mass of feathers and blood.

"A tad dramatic," Lem observed.

"Already, there's been talk about the noble families not being aligned with Bren Caius," Tomas said. "Someone has been careless, boasting about plans that have not yet come to fruition."

"It doesn't take a master from Sage Hall to see that either the noble families or the guildmasters will benefit from this war. It's only a matter of choosing sides. The guildmasters of the north have already committed their full resources to Bren Caius. It's obvious where that leaves us. No one ratted us out. People will put it together."

Once, twice, the roosters collided. And as soon as the fight had started, it ended. One remained on the ground, a clump of matted feathers. The surviving rooster brought its bladed gaffs deep into the fallen foe, unaware the threat was gone. Some of the spectators cheered. Some groaned. Coin was counted and exchanged.

"We have a person in Bren's army who is loyal to our families," Henrik said. "The war mage, Aubec Skarsol. He says Bren Caius does not regard Gandryll's nobility at all. The general's too busy fighting a war."

"Why would Aubec help us?" Tomas asked. "He's a man of honor. He wouldn't associate with conspirators."

"Aubec doesn't know what we are," Henrik said. "I told him we wanted to support the high general but had been spurned as monarchists—which *is* true—and thus, I asked him to keep us informed merely so we could serve the greater good with our resources."

"Salt the lie with truth." Tomas took it all in. "If Aubec uncovers our ill intent and informs Bren Caius, we've failed."

"No, not failure. The plan just gets bloodier, uglier." Henrik laughed weakly, amused by the possibility. "We pour poison at the dinner feasts. We slit throats in the night. Our ancestors rose to power through such means. We can do the same. The general is a good general—but if it must be that way, then so be it."

"That does not reassure me, Henrik."

"My apologies, Tomas. Didn't you say what we're doing is risky? How do you want me to reassure you? Shall we hold hands at the gallows or offer dulcet words of friendship before we are banished?"

"I don't need you to laugh away the danger, but I need to know that I'm in league with competent people who are committed to the cause."

The ragged men returned to the pit to reclaim their dead and damaged roosters. The loser was grabbed unceremoniously by the neck and tossed onto a pile of other chicken carcasses from previous matches. Flies buzzed. The victor was handled more carefully, if only because he still had razor-sharp gaffs fixed to his legs, and the handler didn't want to be the rooster's second victim. After the roosters were removed, a boy entered the pit with a straw broom and swept the area of feathers and blood, smoothing it over for the next match.

"Do you know of my brother, the knight, Owyn Oldcastle?" Lem asked.

"A large man who lived an even larger life," Tomas replied.

"Indeed," Lem said. "Did you know he was a friend to Bren Caius during her last years in Eloe Vale?" Lem waited for an answer, but there was none. "You did not because she rejected him. Shamed him. He adored her, treated her like his daughter. Every day, every night, they convened at the tavern to drink and eat and make merry. The way Oldcastle spoke of those days, you'd think he encased the memories of her in amber. But once Bren gained the favor of Marcus Tom, those days ended. Marcus Tom needed a successor, so he could retire from being the high general and focus on his true passion: poetry. For Bren's part, she saw a ladder. She could become the great Bren Caius she always wanted to be, leaving Oldcastle behind. Oldcastle died soon after she marched from Eloe Vale. But I will not forget him."

"Nor I," Henrik said. "Bren should not outlive Good Owyn Oldcastle by so many days."

"We shall not forget Oldcastle," Tomas said. He held out his hand and the other two took it. They stared at one another, judging their fortitude. "I'll send provisions to Kret's legion this afternoon. I'll include a wax-sealed message that Gandryll's gates will be opened for them."

Once the pit was swept, two more roosters were brought

out. More slips of paper with bets marked on them changed hands.

* * *

The heel of Oren's boot was on the throat of a gasping gnoll. Oren shifted his weight. The gnoll's neck crunched.

"Aaaooh!" Oren hooted with delight. The dead gnoll was mashed to pulp with additional stomps from Oren's boot. The head and upper torso folded in on itself.

Undistracted, even during his mid-battle revels, Oren swung his two-handed sword at another approaching gnoll, sending him to the ground as well. Oren stepped forward and gave that one a swift kick, turning the gnoll's head completely around.

If bloodshed was a banquet, Oren was feasting.

Pikemen advanced cautiously, closing off any retreat from this straggling warband.

Aubec watched at a distance with his arms folded. This warband was the fourth one they had intercepted on the way to Pynne's Field. Aubec had already expended most of his spells for the day on those previous groups. He would occasionally lift his hand to swipe left and then right, creating shimmering force fields to protect the soldiers from any attacks.

The last year of the war had been like this. Bren would scout with Ruth, finding warbands that had broken away from the larger army. Even though gnolls were pack animals, Kret's legion was too large to be considered a pack. They routinely separated to raid and hunt on their own. Bren would move on these groups, striking fast, overwhelming them, and moving on. Bren was using the strategy Kret had devised against the peasant villages, but against the gnolls. Kret's legion was stronger as a unified front, but it wasn't in their nature. With each warband, they came closer to Kret's unified army.

Yulie approached Aubec with a chalice on a silver tray. Her red curls bobbed. She was poised and indifferent to the violence around her.

"Wine, prince?"

"Yes, please. Thank you, child."

Aubec took the chalice and sipped at the red wine. He nodded in approval, set the chalice back on the tray, and continued his warding spells. "Child?"

"Yes, prince?"

"Aren't you afraid to be this close to the gnolls?"

Oren burst through a cluster of gnolls, tossing them in every direction. The pikeman followed, finishing the gnolls lying on the ground.

"I'm not afraid as long as Bren Caius is here. She will protect me."

"Would an army need courage if they had faith like yours?"

"It's not for me to say." With a slight curtsy, Yulie excused herself and walked to the back where the other attendants and the wounded waited with the supplies and pack animals.

As Aubec watched the skirmish, he thought about last night's conversation. The bards must be so thankful their names rhymed—Bren and Oren—for their songs would always be sung together.

Bren Caius wore her plate armor with its blinding brilliance, chainmail coif, and kettle helmet. She fought while astride her horse, swinging her sword down upon the disoriented gnolls.

The soldiers lingered behind Oren and Bren, waiting for

the easy kill. They depended on Aubec's magic to create a safe place for battlefield bravery. It made sense. Here was a mage who could cause fire to erupt around the enemy and protective shields to surround the allies, and here was a Raustfweg warrior who could break any shield wall and plow any field of combatants like they were stalks of wheat for the harvest. Then Bren Caius herself, she embodied perfection while wielding her sword. Why did the common foot soldier need courage? They could cower behind Bren, Oren, and Aubec like children clinging to their parents. Aubec saw it so plainly now. The words in Bren's tent took shape. Cowardice guided their hearts. And they would mutiny if Bren took the slightest step back. The war had gone on too long, and these soldiers didn't have any courage left—not to face Kret and his full army.

* * *

Four warbands were enough. Bren Caius decided they were done for the day. She didn't want to move hastily and find their dwindling army marching straight into a sea of gnolls. Here, they were safe. The soldiers wandered languidly about the campsite, which was nothing more than a field of mud and flattened grass. Bren had doffed her armor before the tent had been raised. She sat on the ground, rolling her shoulders back to ease the ache. A soldier nearby dug at the ground with an axe blade to make a fire pit. He had a pile of stones to form the ridge and a stack of small twigs as kindling. Something caught his attention. He looked past Bren Caius and pointed.

"High general, you have a visitor."

A priest of Tian approached. She walked toward Bren Caius with an air of calm determination. A confused guard followed behind explaining that she couldn't simply walk up to the high general without an invitation or diplomatic cause. The priest ignored the guard. She had a dragon sigil tattoo along her neck and short spiky hair. Both the tattoo and the hair style were common to the priests of Tian. Her golden eyeliner gave her eyes a wild and alluring look. She wore a linen blouse with flared sleeves and laces across the front. Bren was moved by her savage beauty and power, which radiated from her.

The priest stopped in front of Bren and bowed in respect. Bren, who was still sitting, did not return the gesture. Instead, she waved off the guard and shook her head to indicate she was displeased with his uselessness.

"I haven't met many Tian priests this far from the city. What brings you here?"

"Tian cares for people wherever they are." The priest spoke tenderly.

"The named goddess of luck, mischief, and misfortune. I never thought of Tian as a caring deity."

"Fortune is fickle. So are the cares of this world." The priest stood over Bren. "They call me Hild."

Bren had to crane her neck to look at the priest. With a grunt, the general got to her feet. Bren towered nearly a handspan over her, but she felt small in front of the priest.

"Hild, what brings you to my camp?"

"I'm here because this afternoon, one of your soldiers raided a village not far from here. Your soldier cleaned out our storehouse. He also looted some other valuables. This war has brought famine, and what little food we have, we ration. Any theft causes greater suffering among these people."

If it had been anyone else, Bren Caius would have sent them away. But there was something about this woman.

"That's quite an accusation," said Bren. "Could you describe one of the looted items so I can verify if my soldier did it?"

"One of the stolen items was a silver plate with etchings of the four seasons. There's a farmer toiling in each vignette. Find that and you'll find the one responsible."

"Oren!" Bren shouted.

Oren was already standing by her, but Bren hadn't noticed. She jumped when he spoke.

"General?"

"Search the soldiers and their tents. If you find a silver plate among the personal items, bring that soldier to me."

Bren glared at Hild as her way to say, "Are you satisfied?" The priest, hands pressed together, bowed once more.

It didn't take long for Oren to find the thief. He returned to Bren, dragging the wide-eyed soldier behind him. Oren held the silver plate in the other hand. Oren looked like a dog that had caught a rabbit. So proud to complete the task. And like an ensnared rabbit, the soldier struggled against Oren's iron grip.

"Here's the one you're looking for. His name is Bardol of Ryvenmoor."

"From the southern plains?" Bren evaluated the soldier with disappointment. "Ryvenmoor is rich in cattle, beasts in high demand. You can't find them anywhere else in the world. Why do you need silver?"

Bardol did not answer. He had no good response, no honest response to absolve him.

"Hang him outside the camp," Bren said and then walked away, "until death."

If it were possible, Bardol's eye bulged even more. Now he found his words. "What? No! This—you can't. This is insane."

Oren motioned to a guard near him to fetch a rope. Oren then dragged Bardol back through the camp. The other soldiers stepped back, forming a path for Oren. They looked in horror as Bardol cried and screamed.

"You can't do this! I'm a soldier. I, I, I volunteered for this position! I serve Bren Caius. Bren the, the, the beloved!"

This was the first time Bren was ever called "Bren the Beloved." The name would be invoked ironically among the soldiers. The nickname stuck, but its origin faded away.

Aubec rushed across the camp to Bren. He did his best to intercede for Bardol. Hild scowled at the mage, and Bren took note of it. "Bren, the rule of law is clear! The penalty for theft is paid in *coin*." Aubec followed behind Bren and Hild as they walked. Aubec was perplexed by the appearance of this new priestly advisor. He stumbled over his recitation. "For the farming class, it's the return of the item, plus five, no, ten times its worth. And for the merchant class, the returned item, plus—plus twice times its worth. Then, for nobility, the return of the item as well as a formal writ of apology to be posted in the guildhall. The law—"

"Does that seem like justice to you?" Bren snapped at Aubec, but she would not look at him. She spoke while facing forward and walking back to her tent. "A different standard for each class? The wealthiest, who are most capable of restitution, pay nothing. A meaningless apology."

"Losing your standing with the guildmasters is far from meaningless."

"I wonder who wrote that law? Nobles."

"My family comes from nobility. The lineage of the Skarsol family can be traced to Siljard, the first king of northeast Amon, one of the original forty-seven anointed." Aubec strained to keep his composure. He raged inside. "My family offered to fund you, but you rejected them. Perhaps the soldiers wouldn't steal if we paid them a fair wage."

"I remember your family's offer." Bren stopped walking and faced Aubec. "My reasoning was given to you in private to save your family from embarrassment."

"You didn't want to accept coin from monarchists. You won't take my coin, but you'll accept my spellcraft. Now, will you accept my counsel? The law does not require a thief to forfeit their life."

"The crime isn't thievery." Bren put her hands to her forehead in disbelief that they were even having this argument. "The crime is desertion. While we were fighting gnolls, he left the battle to raid the people we're trying to protect. That is much more than thievery. So much more! Is this one of your cowardly archers? How useful are they if they walk away from the fight?"

"Bardol," Aubec sighed, realizing Bren Caius didn't know the people who fought under her command, not their names or their positions. "Bardol serves as a foot soldier."

"Not an archer. Then you won't mind too much if we hang him?"

Aubec considered a reply, but Bren could not be swayed. Her eyes were storms of fire.

Aubec walked away. His red cape shifted with a snap.

"I serve Bren the Beloved! I serve Bren the Beloved!" Tears flowed down Bardol's face. Oren tied a noose with one hand while holding Bardol with his other. He could've snapped

Bardol's neck with his bare hand, but Bren wanted a hanging. So, he tied the noose.

"Please! My family!" Bardol's words were barely discernible as he blubbered and sobbed. "I haven't seen my youngest child. Her name is Olivette. She was born right after I joined the campaign in Asher. I need to see my children again. I need to see my wife. You can't kill me."

These words caught Oren's attention. "I assure you, I can." Oren spoke quietly, but the words cut through the assembled crowd.

Oren pulled the noose over Bardol's head. Bardol squealed. He slapped at Oren's arm.

"I can pay the family ten times, twenty times the cost of that plate. I will pay anything." Oren threw the other end of the rope over a thick tree limb. "Nonononono—"

The other soldiers, Aubec among them, pressed closer to watch the execution. Silent, unsure. Friends of Bardol wept. All the soldiers shifted in discomfort. Each knew this was wrong, but they were helpless to stop it.

Oren pulled at the rope, dragging Bardol along the ground. The rope cut into Bardol's neck. His face flushed red—his mouth gaping, a desperate wordless plea for air. No sound came, only a horrified look on his swollen face. Oren pulled again, raising Bardol into the air. Bardol swung from the noose. His legs kicked wildly. One kick connected with Oren's chest. Oren frowned in annoyance. He pulled on the rope, then gave it slack and yanked it. Bardol went up and then down. His neck cracked. His head fell to the side, lying flat against his shoulder. Bardol was dead. When Oren was satisfied, he let go of the rope. Bardol's body fell to the ground.

Mutterings of injustice spread through the crowd. Oren

dusted his hands, another job done. He stepped through the crowd, ever faithful, returning to Bren.

Ruth landed beside Bardol's body, flapped her wings, and hopped about, appearing to investigate the grizzly scene—more like a curious buzzard than a barn owl.

Bren opened her eyes as her natural senses returned to her. Hild watched Bren with interest—the golden eyeliner perfectly framing those dark eyes.

"Be satisfied, priest. The thief is dead. And if it were possible, I am even more despised among my troops. We are outnumbered by Kret. And less one foot soldier by your request."

Yulie was already there to hand Bren a glass of wine. She offered a glass to Hild, which she accepted. They entered the tent, now raised and tethered.

"I never asked you to execute him."

"Didn't you though? You spoke of famine and rationing and suffering. You came into my camp saying my soldiers ignore my orders. How did you expect me to respond?"

Bren sat upon a floor pillow. Hild joined her.

"I expect fair judgment," Hild looked around the large tent, taking in the lavish setting. "Nothing more."

"Clearly, you've never fought in any wars."

"And neither did you until this war."

Bren took a drink and set down her cup. "I've seen combat. Ever since I was a little child, I've been fighting."

"So the bards and poets would claim."

Sitting next to Hild, Bren felt a rush she only experienced on the battlefield, a sense of her mortality.

"Who are you?"

"I already told you. I'm a priest of Tian."

"Why else are you here?"

"To give you what you need."

Bren tilted her head. She was unsure where this was going, but Bren decided to speak the truth.

"I need your wisdom. The war has gone on too long. My soldiers are cowards. They are exposed, stripped of the delusions that bolster bravery. They are tired. Aubec, Oren, and I cannot fight this war ourselves. Yet the soldiers keep waiting for us to fight for them."

"When the most powerful person in Amon comes to a Tian priest for counsel, we know these are uncertain times. If you want my counsel, to start . . . " Hild leaned forward and took Bren's cup from her, just as Yulie was about to refill it. "Try not getting drunk tonight. The bards and poets do not speak of your drunkenness, but everyone else does. Tomorrow might be the most important day in your life. If you confront Kret, and your soldiers expect you to fight for them, do it without a hangover."

"A Tian priest advising sobriety. That's new."

"You can drink once the war is over."

"In that case, let's end the war tonight."

"You say the soldiers are waiting for you to fight for them," Hild ventured into the crux of her visit. "But don't you want to face Kret Bonebreaker in single combat? A duel for the fate of Amon."

Bren eyed Hild. "How do you know what I want?"

"Tian has blessed my dreams with moments from your life, both what has happened and what will happen."

"You are more than a priest. You're a prophet. Why me?"

Hild laughed at the question. "You know why. I've never met anyone so aware of their own importance. The gods don't send visions of people who leave no mark on the world. But also, I believe Tian is a great admirer."

The stained glass in the hanging lamps caught the daylight in such a way that it cast various rays of color across the interior of the tent. The effect was beautiful and otherworldly.

"The next time you light a candle and say your prayers, you can let Tian know Kret won't face me in single combat unless the war has turned in my favor, and he sees it as his best opportunity."

"Kret is not staying in Pynne's Field for long. He's heading to Gandryll. If you can keep him from getting there, he'll take greater risks to push through. You'll get the fight you've been wanting."

* * *

Tomas arrived in his carriage to the spring pond near Pynne's Field. The horses pulling the carriage had been uneasy as they approached. Even from this distance, Tomas could hear the yips and howls of the gnoll army encamped nearby. Tomas was told to leave the carriage here and to walk the rest of the way.

His hands shook as he removed the vial from his coat pocket. The instructions were clear. He must apply the contents of the vial to his hair and neck if he hoped to encounter the camp unharmed.

Tomas removed the cap and gagged at the pungent smell of rotten fish and chamber lye. He gagged a second time and held it away from him. Even the horses reacted to the smell. He wasn't sure if he could do this. But if he failed to deliver the provisions, how would he explain it to Henrik and Lem? All their plans would be ruined.

He held his breath and poured out the vial into his open palm. The solution was brown with congealed bits. The smell hit with more force than before. He retched and could taste the vomit in the back of his throat. As instructed, he rubbed the substance into his hair and along the back of his neck. It warmed on his skin and then burned. Tomas whimpered. He had never felt so terrible before. He was dizzy and sick and nauseous, but he found the strength to get out of the carriage. Dragging one foot, then the other, he walked the dirt path toward a rock-strewn hill around the bend into the heart of the camp.

Before Tomas could even register what was happening, he was surrounded by gnolls, mangy canine-like creatures. They sniffed at him, pushing their snouts on him and aggressively examining his peculiar scent. When they caught a whiff of the horrid substance from the vial, each gnoll became more curious, sniffing with greater interest—but ultimately, they left Tomas alone, backing away and allowing him to continue to the center of camp.

Goblins, smaller and hunchbacked, green and wart-covered, waddled among the gnolls. They observed Tomas hungrily, mouths parting in wide, sharp-toothed grins. They spoke among themselves, giggling and staring at Tomas. Their attention made him uncomfortable.

The whole experience of entering the camp was so overwhelming, he didn't even notice he had been crying. Tomas was a noble. Everywhere he went, he was respected and given the courtesy of his station. Everywhere, except here. He felt vulnerable, like cooked meat on a spit, and he did not like this feeling one bit.

Away from the cluster, Tomas saw a group of trolls. The gaunt nightmares appeared to glide in their movements, a dance of nonsensical gestures and motions. Their movements were hypnotic. Something about them denied comprehension. One was much closer than Tomas realized. Tomas jumped when it appeared right over him, but the troll continued on its way, taking long steps, showing no concern for the man from Gandryll. The troll flexed its long fingers, razor like and capable of removing Tomas's head with ease.

"Gods protect me," was all Tomas could say. This was what awaited Bren Caius and her remaining soldiers. How could they stand a chance?

Farther off were the ogres, thick and muscular, taller than any human. They were slumped to the ground, leaning against one another, asleep. The face of each ogre was exaggerated and expressive, a continuously furrowed brow, nostrils and lips flared in a snarl. They were dreaming of violence.

At the center of the camp was the general's tent. The only tent. The other monsters, it seemed, slept on the ground. Outside the tent, Speck waited for Tomas. His hands behind his back. He rocked back and forth on his feet. With this goblin's white eyes, Tomas could not tell if Speck was looking at him or past him. And then he spoke.

"A steady journey, Tomas of Umber."

"Why couldn't you meet me at the pond?"

"Let's try again. A steady journey, Tomas of Umber."

"And a clear path," Tomas replied wearily.

"Much better." Speck walked around Tomas, swaying as he moved. "You are more than a guest. You are a partner with us in the slaughter of your own people. Exciting, isn't it? We may look gruesome, but we know who the real monster is." Speck pointed at Tomas to remove any doubt. Tomas felt his heart sink. Everything felt wrong, but there was no backing out.

"I brought a fourth of the supplies in my carriage," Tomas said. "My servants are transporting the rest this afternoon. They will unload the crates at the pond and then travel back to Gandryll. Everything you requested."

"The magnesia powder?"

"It's in a sealed barrel in my carriage, marked with a white annulet."

"Good. And the gates?"

"They will be open when you arrive." Tomas reached into his pouch and pulled out the waxed-sealed letter, which outlined the arrangements. His hand shook so violently, it appeared as if he were waving a white flag at the goblin. "We've reserved the west end of Gandryll for your lodgings."

"That," Speck shook his head, "was not part of the deal. We'll lodge where we please. We'll take what we please. We'll do what we please. And in exchange, your families may live and thrive." Speck grabbed the sealed letter from Tomas and let it drop to the ground.

"Yes, sir." Tomas could feel the sweat running down the back of his neck, and the burning of the vial's contents returned.

Speck gestured to the tent.

"Would you like to meet Kret Bonebreaker?"

"Now?" The name of the gnoll warlord shook Tomas to his core. A deeper level of panic, which Tomas didn't think was possible, overcame him. It felt like he was sinking into the ground.

"He's waiting for you."

* * *

Corrinae, the daughter of Tomas and Beatrice Umber, stood in front of a full-length mirror. The mirror had a dark wood frame inlaid with mother-of-pearl. The gift came from a distant relative of the Welton family, some three generations ago. Corrinae admired her green dress, which her maid was buttoning in the back. Corrinae was old enough to be considered an adult, but just barely. She was still a child in many ways —too young to live on her own or manage a household, too young to know her heart.

Corrinae fussed with her long auburn hair. She practiced her smile and tilted her head from one side to the other.

"Please stay still, m'lady. These buttons are stubborn." Lefrith, the maid, shook her head, amused by Corrinae's high-spirited, restless nature. Lefrith loved Corrinae as she would've loved her own children had they survived infancy. The pox outbreaks in Gandryll cruelly coincided with every time Lefrith had given birth. A third child gone, and she committed herself full-time to the care of the Umber household. She had been Corrinae's wet nurse. She cared for Corrinae her whole life. "M'lady, be still."

"But Lefrith, I must look perfect for when Bren Caius arrives."

"If Bren Caius arrives, yes. If. I heard about your mother's scheming. But it looks as though a final battle to decide the war is to be waged in Pynne's Field. If Kret Bonebreaker is victorious, we pack you in our fastest ship and send you to Hazelef to live with your aunt—then we pray there's a Gandryll left for you to return to. However, if Bren Caius is victorious, the Umber family will hold a feast in her honor."

"And?" Corrinae urged.

"And," Lefrith sighed, "Beatrice will introduce you to the high general and mention that you and Halsten of Cain-Oldcastle, with such good lineage and influence, are eligible in every way a man and woman can be. After all, you are both inclined to the *mark* and the *score*—"

Corrinae wrinkled her nose at the crude slang. "Lefrith!"

"We all know about the high general's sexual appetite. It's better to let Bren Caius know, straightway, how the arrangement can work, if she is interested." Lefrith patted Corrinae's cheek. "Your mother will also remind her that a union with two southern houses would be to her advantage. Marriage with one house is an alliance. Marriage with two houses? That's an enduring legacy. Caius would become the most powerful name in Amon for generations."

"Lefrith, I swear, you overhear too much."

"Then tell your mother to talk softer."

Lefrith had watched Corrinae grow from a happy child into a wide-eyed young woman, one who believed in romantic stories of courtly love between a princess and her knight, someone who could rescue the maiden from the tower. Corrinae had spent her whole life in the Umber manor, a short distance outside of Gandryll. She lived a life of comfort, ease, and extravagance. And still, she would sit on the cushion at the open window. Her head propped on her hands, her elbows upon the windowsill. She would sigh deeply and dream of a better life. How Corrinae could imagine a world greater than the one she already lived in was a mystery to Lefrith. But

Lefrith knew to never doubt the wild ambitions of pampered people.

"Lefrith, can I try on the blue dress? The new one that shipped from Yére. The tailor promised me his most elegant design."

"Yes, m'lady." Lefrith walked across to the armoire and searched through Corrinae's dresses. "May I ask, m'lady, do you think Bren Caius will be victorious? The talk on the street is that the Northern Army is outnumbered, and that it's foolish to face those hideous beasts on the open field of battle."

"I'm certain Bren will be victorious." Corrinae looked from her mirror to the window, half expecting to see the battle in the east garden. "I just am."

Lefrith held the blue dress over Corrinae's head. Corrinae raised her arms, and Lefrith pulled it down over her.

"I'm afraid that 'I just am' wouldn't get you a pint at the tavern. You'll need to do better."

Corrinae was always amused when Lefrith challenged her.

"You've heard the legends." Corrinae brushed her hair while Lefrith shook the wrinkles out of the dress. "If even half of Bren's life story is nothing more than the inventions of drunks and liars, I'd say she is blessed by fate to be victorious. She is certainly more cunning. She will devise a plan to defeat Kret Bonebreaker."

"Do you swear by it?"

"I swear by my hand." Corrinae held up her right hand. "If I'm wrong, you can cut it off."

"Your hand, m'lady?"

"And all my fingers and the nails upon them, too. You can take my whole arm. My foot as well."

"M'lady, I don't know what I'd do with all your spare parts. They work better as a coordinated set."

"Take it all. Cut out my heart, too. I won't need it if Bren Caius should fall in battle."

The playfulness left the room, flying out the window and dissipating into the night sky.

For years, Corrinae had heard nobles talk about what a good match she would be for the high general. Corrinae never thought to ask why. Matters of court were tangled affairs of power and influence—something for parents to negotiate and work through. Corrinae only knew there was no name in Amon greater than Caius.

The nobles worried about Bren's opposition to the peerage and the whole system of titled lands leased to farmers. Bren had come from humble origins, and the nobles were afraid she'd burn down their feudal ways, if given the chance. To the nobles, Bren Caius was a problem. They wanted to resolve this problem the way they tried to resolve everything—with strategic marriages. Almost every noble couple could point to the particular political strife that led to their union. But Corrinae did not see the politics. She had fallen in love with an idea.

Lefrith placed her hands on Corrinae's shoulders to comfort her.

"It'll be all right. Your knight will come."

* * *

At the end of the scene, the actors playing Corrinae and the maid were statues on the stage, a tableau of motherly care. There was no applause, no laughter. During this quiet moment, the audience reflected on great love among Corrinae, Halsten, and Bren Caius. The window—nothing more than cloth draped over the curtain with the image of a window stitched on it—was especially meaningful. After the death of Bren Caius, Corrinae and Halsten would both fall from that same window. A terrible accident.

The actors dragged out the tableau a bit too long, reveling in their dramatic triumph. Many troupes played this scene for laughs. The flighty, spoiled aristocrat and the common maid trading witty jokes about young wives trying to please their spouses. The jokes were obscene and predictable musings on a lonely bed turning into a crowded bed. The innocent noble would be revealed as a scandalously amorous woman and the maid blushed at every word. But the actors in this troupe played it with unexpected depth.

Pike walked onto the stage, signaling for the actors to exit. They had their moment and then some. For Ekor, watching from behind the curtain, this subtle exchange was one of the more dramatic moments. Would the actors obey their leader, or would they bask in the attention for as long as they could?

On this day, the actors relented.

Corrinae had another scene at the end of the play, and the maid was also cast as one of the soldiers who appeared later. Both seemed satisfied with their moments on the stage.

"Ekor. You're on soon. Get ready." Jamison, the actor playing Kret, stood over Ekor. He was already a tall man, but the stilts wrapped in fur made him comically oversized. Jamison had a gentle disposition and a high voice that made him sound like a bird chirping.

"I've been ready for hours now." Ekor gestured at his

squirrel costume. "Do you think I wear this because it's the fashion of the day?"

Even though Jamison was three times the age and twice the height of Ekor—without the stilts—he still wilted at Ekor's sarcasm. "I'm terribly sorry, young sir. You know how nervous I get before my big scene. The crowd has been waiting and waiting for Kret. I want to make a good impression."

Ekor knew that if the play had one flaw, there was too much talking and not enough fighting. The characters prattle on about how horrible and monstrous Kret is, but do you ever see him? Not until the last act.

"You will. You'll do great," Ekor comforted Jamison. "Listen. There's a group of children on the left side of the stage. They've been jumping at everything. When you go out there, give them a big growl, loud and mean."

"Thanks, I appreciate it." Jamison sheepishly returned the compliment. "And they're gonna love you."

Ekor shook his head. "I have the dumbest part in the whole play. We all know it. But it doesn't matter. Someday, it'll be my sister's role, and I can play the goblin mage or a gnoll."

Ekor and Jamison heard laughter and shifted their attention to Pike on the stage.

"Now, good audience, I will ask you to conjure in your mind that it is nighttime," Pike held her hands out. She wandered the small stage, blind in the fabricated darkness. "The pouring darkness floods the land. Don't wait for me to guide you. Imagine it! Imagine! We are in darkness." Pike said each word with slow deliberateness to emphasize the hopeless state. She moved her hands from her face. "From the camp, you can hear the typical sounds of people settling in for the night. Muted conversations. The crackle of fire. The crickets' stridulation, humming in unison. Horses snort and neigh. A single armorer hammers, mending rivets, a high-pitched clang, clang, clang. Dreadful notes of preparation. The two armies—Bren's and Kret's—are close. The soldiers think they can hear the other camp nearby, no less than a mile, two miles, perhaps. And the sentinels of Amon sense they are mercilessly outnumbered. The campfire only illuminates the faces of soldiers leaning toward each other. Do you see the many floating heads, like a sacrifice, a mass execution at the chopping block of history?"

For Ekor, this monologue was his favorite. Pike would work the audience to get a laugh, and then, she could shift the tone to move everyone to tears. She was quite gifted. As the Chorus, she kept the audience off guard. She believed her job was one of setting and subverting expectation. They all knew the story of Bren Caius. The Chorus could play into that, and if she could keep them guessing—the story would feel new every time, and the story would maintain its power. She could keep the audience engaged.

What Pike did next was always shocking. She dropped pretense and shifted to a natural, conversational tone. She acted as if she broke from her character, but this was part of the act.

"I—hold on," Pike paused. "I need a moment." The audience looked at one another, confused. The patron furrowed his brow. Was the play over? Pike held up her hand to him, reassuring. "I swear this hasn't happened before." Ekor grinned. This scene always happened. It was in the script.

"We've performed *War of the Hounds* countless times, and what we give you is a facsimile, a heightened reality, but think for a moment. This moment happened. In another time, in another place. Common people took up arms to fight a demon and his horde, knowing they were outnumbered, knowing they might not survive. And yet—" Pike's voice cracked, not an overwrought cry, but a much more realistic moment. Her performance was a type of subtle acting the audience had never seen before, the opposite of the scene between Corrinae and Lefrith. Perhaps Pike did it on purpose. At times, she pushed her actors for this new realism. She had become bored with the traditional forms. Pike regained her composure.

"And yet, this brave band stayed to finish the fight. And what did Bren do? She walked from watch to watch, a smile for each soldier, calling them sibling, kin, and friend." Pike had no way of knowing what happened that evening, but the audience accepted her version. "Each one comforted by her presence." In a burst of enthusiasm, Pike returned to her larger persona. "A little touch of Bren in the night!" She made a spectacularly obscene gesture, one which Ekor's father said he would explain someday. The audience blushed and gasped. Many laughed.

"I'm sorry. I'm sorry. I've delayed long enough. Pynne's Field awaits. Sit and see, mind the true things despite our mockery." Pike sighed. "Shall we continue with the play?"

* * *

Inside the general's tent, the hanging lanterns were lit to keep the night from invading. Bren, Aubec, Oren, and Hild—the newest advisor—all stood around a crudely drawn map. Bren held a dowel rod, which she used to indicate strategic locations.

Aubec and Oren both stared at Hild, baffled by her presence. It had always been the three of them. And now, there was this strange addition, a priest. She was a priest of Tian, no less —the goddess of mischief and trickery. Hild stood close to

Bren. She occasionally whispered in Bren's ear. To which Bren would give a nod as she pondered this secret wisdom.

When Aubec finally demanded to know why this outsider was with them, Bren simply said that three was a cursed number, and she felt one more person on this council would be ideal. Aubec questioned the prudence of taking advice from a priest of Tian. But Bren reminded Aubec that Tian served the gamblers, the long shots, and the hopeless cases. No other god was better suited for their cause.

Even though Aubec believed the gods were best left alone in all matters, he agreed that they needed some luck.

It had been a long day. Yulie yawned. She approached Bren with a filled cup and a wine bottle.

"Wine, princess?"

Bren shook her head and waved the girl away. Her focus remained on the map. Aubec and Oren looked at each other. They had never seen Bren refuse a drink at any time, day or night. A month ago, Bren had fought while drinking. She held her sword in one hand and a bottle in the other. After that battle, Oren and Aubec had tried to intervene. Oren urged for sensibility. Always take a shield into battle. Aubec pleaded for moderation and decorum. They both left with matching red whelps on their faces—the shape of Bren's hand. Bren made her opinion clear on sensibility, moderation, and decorum.

"You sent Ruth to scout again," Aubec said. "What did you find?"

"Kret's legion set camp outside of Pynne's Field, not far from us," Bren yawned to match Yulie's. The hour was late. She was tired, but no sleep would come tonight. Hild rubbed her back to comfort her. "As you saw in Ilden, they're cutting down trees without any intention of using the timber. They travel in haste and stop only to clear a portion of the forest. They're now done and will continue west to Gandryll."

"How do you know they're traveling to Gandryll?" Aubec could not hide the worry in his voice.

Instead of Bren answering, Hild cut in.

"I saw a vision of the hounds marching to Gandryll, and the path is blocked. There will be a final battle with Bren killing Kret, but it's unclear. Also, on another day, Kret will kill Bren. Both are true, absolutely true. I can't reconcile them, but for tomorrow, fortune is on our side."

"I don't remember asking you," Aubec snapped at her. "If I need someone to share their hallucinations, I'll send for you."

"If we attack from the east," Bren ignored Aubec and returned to her map, "the terrain offers no positional advantage for either side, but since they have the numbers, it favors them. If we attack from the west, at this narrow gap in the forest, it favors us. The choice is clear. We attack from the west."

"They have no cause to fight us on this front," Aubec said. "They can move east and continue raiding along the coast."

"Aubec is right," Oren conceded. "It'd be foolish for Kret to fight us on the west. That choke point gives us a great advantage."

"Except, since they are in a hurry to get to Gandryll," Hild responded, "they must go this way."

"If they are going to Gandryll," Aubec emphasized.

"Since they are going to Gandryll," Bren corrected. "This is the fight we want. We position the archers along the tree line, but hidden further back, on either side. Aubec will cast his fire spells at their back ranks to make retreat more difficult."

"When their numbers dwindle," Oren pointed to the

battlefield, "Kret might request single combat to resolve the battle. Are you prepared to have me fight as your champion?"

"I will be facing Kret Bonebreaker," Bren said, unsurprised by Oren's attempt to take her place. "I'm the better fighter."

"I'm stronger."

"And Kret is stronger than you," said Hild. "What of it? We're not competing to see who can toss a stone the farthest. All Bren needs to do is deliver a mortal cut."

"That's all?" Oren laughed at her reductive conclusion. "And if Bren dies, what will happen to Amon?"

"If I die, you have my permission to kill Kret." Bren said. She noted Oren's approval. An acceptable compromise. "And if I die, Aubec, you will make sure the nobles of Gandryll are the first to know."

Bren wanted to get a reaction from Aubec. He did react, but in subtle ways only a close friend would notice. His countenance was blank, strained in its neutrality. Bren could tell Aubec didn't want her to see any reaction, which was itself a reaction. He took a deep breath, stalling for a response.

Bren had her suspicions about why Kret was set on traveling to Gandryll. Before their meeting, Hild told Bren that the nobles of the city had no love for her. And why would they? They wanted a crown on *her* head, so she could prop *them* up with titles—to further a system that stole the land from people who worked it—through deeds and writs signed by her hand. She didn't want it, and the nobles took this rejection as a personal attack. Aubec was from a noble family and had his connections.

She had wondered about Gandryll. Would the nobles—the ones Aubec knew and trusted—collude with Kret Bonebreaker? And seeing Aubec stare back at her—not surprised at her words or confused by her accusation—she wondered about him, too.

"I don't know what you're talking about," he said evenly.

"I think you do."

Oren noticed the cold words exchanged between the high general and her war mage. He clenched his fist, ready to strike at Aubec, if given the command.

Hild stepped back.

"If you don't want me here," Aubec said, "if I've done something to lose your trust, you can dismiss me."

"You will stay here and help me," Bren said. "I don't need your undying allegiance. But I do need your spells. Mages are rare. They have one. We have one. The war is lost without you."

Aubec considered Bren's words in silence. Oren looked to Bren with a questioning look, a wordless inquiry to kill Aubec. Bren marveled at Oren's devotion to her. Aubec and Oren had been friends for years. Yet, he would strike Aubec down without another thought if it pleased his general.

"I would urge mercy," Hild advised. "Aubec's fate is already written. He will survive fire and water. In old age, Aubec will die while seeing his own reflection."

Bren shook her head at Oren, signaling to back down.

"I would never betray you," Aubec said, ignoring Hild.

"I'm sure you have your reasons, and they seem honorable to you. If Kret wins the battle, scurry off to Gandryll. The nobles can pursue whatever treaty they think will preserve Amon and its people."

"You are Amon," Oren said defiantly.

Bren smiled. Her owl flapped from its perch as if in agreement. "That sort of talk is dangerous. And it's not why we're here." Bren wanted a glass of wine. She felt jittery without it, but she pressed on. "Oren, before you retire for the night, have the captains divide their troops into four groups. There's no need to break camp." Bren looked to Hild, and the priest put her hand on Bren's shoulder. Aubec and Oren bristled at the overly familiar gesture. "You'll stay at the camp. Make your offerings and pray for us. We'll leave everything here—except armor, weapons, and water. When the birds chirp before the sunrise, we march to the western front indicated on the map." Bren touched the dowel to four places on the large parchment. "The archers need to take their positions first along the northern and southern sections of the forest. They stay low and hidden. Oren takes the vanguard. Aubec, if you stay at the back, will you still be within range to cast those spells at their rear guard?"

"It's a bit far," Aubec admitted.

"How about if you stay with the archers?"

"That would work. If Speck doesn't know where I'm casting from, that should make it harder to counter. But it will make our main force a greater target. The choke point works both ways. We can't spread out."

Bren tapped the map emphatically.

"This is a good strategy," Hild said. "Tian favors you in all things."

"There are no perfect plans in combat," Bren said. "Don't lie to the infantry and try to comfort them with false hope. Tomorrow will be a difficult day. We can only hope the other side loses more than we do. Agreed?"

Aubec and Oren studied the map and then looked to Bren in silent accord.

"It's been a long day. We're done here." Bren pointed to the tent flap. Oren and Hild both gave a short bow and walked out. Aubec followed behind him. Bren turned to her cupbearer. "Yulie, you too. I'd like to be alone."

Yulie was confused. Bren rarely dismissed her. Often Bren would pass out drunk and that was the cupbearer's signal she was done for the evening. Most times when Bren was "alone," Yulie was still standing discreetly at the ready within the tent, somewhere in the corner.

"Yes, princess. Thank you."

Yulie walked out of the tent. Her red curls bobbed.

Bren sat down, legs crossed, in the middle of her tent. The beaded trinkets hanging from the canopy roof swayed from the light breeze that snuck in when Yulie left. The flap closed. Bren thought about when she was Yulie's age.

As a child, Bren couldn't control her ability to see through the eyes of animals. Every day was a confusion of flight and climbing, swimming and burrowing, galloping and slithering. Her perspective shifted from one living thing to another. This second sight confused and terrified her.

One moment she was fetching water from the well, outside the town. The next moment, she was racing along the soft forest, trying to escape a predator. The burrow was so close, if only she could make it. The wolf snapped at her. She tried to run, but she was not fast enough. When her sight returned, she was on the ground. Her bucket tipped over, spilling cool water onto the ground and onto herself.

She settled down for the night. She closed her eyes, and she was flying over a field, hunting a field mouse. She swooped down and grabbed at the furry snack—with a squeeze and a squeak, the mouse was dead. Bren woke up in bed, screaming triumphantly. Her mother rushed to her bedside. Bren, still full of predatory rage, attacked her mom.

Another time, she was a deer stepping carefully along a stony brook. Her fawn stood close. The morning fog hung heavy. They both bent down to drink from the stream. Everything was quiet and peaceful. She had never experienced a more perfect moment, and it broke her heart to realize the moment was not hers. It never would be.

Once Bren gained control of the second sight, she became confident and powerful. She was courageous as the bear. She was stealthy like the fox, mischievous like the raccoon. She could seek and gather. She could hunt in a hundred different ways. Not only could she control when and how she reached out, but she also gained a degree of control over the animals. She could never urge them to do something outside of their nature. A badger remained a badger. But Bren could compel the animal to go left, to explore over there, to follow that scent and see where it led.

Her explorations into the minds of different animals lead a pack of curious wolves to her family's doorstep. The story became legend. The most common version of the story was that Bren fought off the wolves with a sling and some rocks. But the real story was even more unbelievable. She dismissed the wolves with a word. She told them to leave, and they did, heads lowered and tails between their legs.

Bren remembered how her parents looked at her, more terrified of the strange little girl in front of them than the wolves at their door, terrified of whatever demon magic she possessed.

They did not know their true daughter.

Bren was delivered as an infant at their front doorstep days after their own child had died in the crib. They decided to raise Bren, but she was not like them. She did not act like them, and she did not look like them. When Bren was older, her adoptive mother told her everything. Her mother even shared how she was tempted to drown Bren in the bath after the wolf incident. In a flat, haunted voice, her mother spoke about the witchery surrounding this strange little girl.

"Don't tell anyone about what you can do." Bren's mother couldn't even look at her. She was either too afraid or too ashamed. "They will not understand. An evil spirit hangs over you, child. We thought you were a gift from the gods, but you are a fey curse. You cursed us. You'll only bring misfortune to the people closest to you."

The young Bren took those words to heart and left her family. She had no wolf pack to protect her. No burrow or nest to hide away in. If she was going to survive, she needed sharp teeth and sharp claws. She needed a sword. At the tavern in Eloe Vale, she won silver from the drunks when she bet she could wrestle a stag to the ground. She used her second sight to convince the beast to lie down. Bren used the coin to buy a sword, and another legendary tale was born.

At the tavern, she met Owyn Oldcastle. He had heard stories about this ferocious young pup, and he had to see her for himself. Owyn Oldcastle had served several different noble households throughout his time as a knight. He had been a great warrior once, but the prolonged peace in that region had dulled his blade. The knight was still beloved by the noble families, but they had no use for him except as an entertaining house guest. His sharp wit served him well in courtly matters. He could talk his way into and out of most problems. As he drank and ate his life away, he became a lamentable relic of a bygone era. The charity of the ruling class ran its course, and Owyn was relegated from the manor to the rookery at the far end of town.

Outcast to outcast, Owyn found Bren, and he became like a father to her. Over the years, he taught her how to sword fight. He gave her the teeth and claws she'd been wanting. And she gave him someone to drink with. There was much laughter and joy in those taverns. They were the happiest days of Bren's life, the days before Bren had to choose between Owyn Oldcastle and becoming high general. Marcus Tom was not a great leader, but Owyn knew Bren could not remain loyal to both. If she stayed, the tavern would be her undoing.

"Don't stoop to be the queen." Owyn set down his drink and looked directly at Bren. He smiled the kindest smile Bren had ever known, and it broke her heart to think of it. "Every generation talks about bringing back the monarchy. Taraki anointed forty-seven monarchs to rule over Efre Ousel. And who're we to disagree? But the gods are idiots. People are idiots. They don't understand!" Owyn spoke in a drunken, slurred voice. Whenever people imitated Owyn behind his back, they stuck out their belly, rubbed it proudly, and slurred their speech. The act was always done as a light jest. Everybody loved Owyn, but there was no doubt what he was. A man killing himself with drink and frivolity. "A monarch'll rule for a few years—most of those years will be fraught—then they'll die. With their death, they hand everything over to their progeny, who'll mess it all up. At best, they're incompetent. At worst, they're capable and corrupt. More strife, more war."

Owyn struggled to dismount from his bar stool. He then

turned to address the whole tavern. He shouted, "A steady journey!"

Everyone there responded affably in unison, "And a clear path!"

"Aye, a clear path to your mother's bed!" Owyn held court with the tavern, just like this, on most nights. "The line's long, but she's worth the wait. Your parents've been kind and accommodating to Old Owyn. I can't entertain like I once did." With the word "entertain," Owyn grabbed at his crotch, and everyone howled with laughter. "So, thank your mothers for me, will you? Will you? Will you?" He pointed to people at the tavern who raised their glasses in good cheer. "But not you," Owyn waved aside one patron. "We might be related. And I won't have anyone talk about your mother that way, especially if it's your dad. And I'm he. Terribly sorry." More laughter. Owyn urged everyone to quiet down, so he could return to his point.

"Bren!" He motioned to Bren, who stood up and took a bow. "Bren's special." Everyone nodded in agreement. "No one can fight like she can. Already, word about her valor—that's a word, right? No one has ever used it to describe me." There were a few laughs in the tavern, but more subdued, as people waited for Owyn to get to his point. "Valor. Courage. Skill. Cunning. Charm. This is what people say of our Bren—except the last bit. No one's ever thought of Bren as charming." Bren playfully slapped at Owyn. "Truly, there's no one greater than Bren. There's been talk in Rhyll about bestowing a surname." Bren had not heard about this. She perked up. "And I should know because I sent the petition. Caius. That's the surname I petitioned for. It wasn't cheap. I had to spend all the coin I've stolen." This was not a joke. The people at the tavern looked among themselves, each wondering if Owyn had stolen from them. "Caius! *Caius* is the Volir word for 'joy' because she's my second greatest joy." Owyn grabbed for his drink to make it clear what his first joy was. "Bren's a gift from the gods. She's like a daughter to me. But with a surname and future glory will come talk of a new royal line. Woeful and inevitable. Let's prepare a throne for Bren. And let her practice saying 'no' to the crown. Restraint, my friends. Restraint is key!" As Owyn spoke, he swung his mug and spilled his drink on the floor. He lost his balance, toppling into Bren, who held him up.

The tavern regulars moved the tables together to create a dais. They set a chair upon it for a throne. A barmaid draped a bear fur over it for greater effect. Owyn regained his balance and offered his hand to lead Bren onto the tables. Everyone cheered. She sat upon the throne.

The cook emerged from the kitchen with a brass colander, which he turned over and handed to Owyn as a makeshift crown. Owyn took the colander with a bow, and then bent his knee, holding it out to Bren.

"Bren, you'll be a legend throughout Amon. Will you also be its queen?"

"Never, Good Owyn. Never. A monarch is a miserable, corrupt creature, far removed from the common folk. Too dishonorable to enjoy life, and yet not dishonorable enough to find themselves in a tavern like this one."

The people in the tavern booed.

"You will never be queen? Never?" Owyn asked, a faint smile on his lips.

"Never!" she bellowed melodramatically.

Everyone erupted with laughter, and they raised their drinks.

Bren looked at her friend Owyn. A tear formed in the corner of her eye. Bren whispered for only Owyn to hear, "Make me an Oldcastle. Make me your daughter. Truly and legally. I don't want to be a Caius. There is no joy without your name."

"You're destined for greater things. Who's Good Owyn? My days are done. You must leave here and find your fame. Banish me." Owyn's voice shook as he spoke.

Bren wiped the tears from her eyes. "I will," she said.

Bren Caius held her kettle helmet, thinking about lost friendships and those days long ago at the Eloe Vale tavern. Surrounded by the glow of lamplight, she placed the helmet on her head, then pressed it down for a snug fit. Not quite a crown, but the helmet represented an office she had been destined to fill.

She was a warrior.

The brimmed steel covering made her look a bit dopey— but it had saved her life on occasion. In battle, she would wear it. Let the artists paint her without one.

Bren closed her eyes. Motes of blue light twinkled, faintly reflecting off the dull helmet. When she could see again, it was through the eyes of a squirrel perched in a tree. The squirrel scampered down the thick rivulets of tree bark to get a better look at the soldiers seated around the campfire.

Haim the archer stared into the fire. His dirty face had lighter streaks from tears earlier in the day. One eye was half red, a burst blood vessel. He told people it was a battle injury. But truthfully, it was from crying.

Across from Haim, an older man sharpened his sword with a whetstone. The periodic scraping noise did not bother anyone. Next to him was a woman, her head shaved to the scalp except for a strip of hair down the middle. She wore an elaborate necklace adorned with coins. A hole was punched in the middle of each coin. A strap of leather threaded them together.

"Tomorrow is it," Haim said. "The last battle. The one we've been dreading. The one we've been wanting."

"Have any of you fought in a battle of this size?" the man sharpening his sword asked. "I've been in skirmishes. Nothing like this."

"None of us are iron-banded," the woman responded. "In Amon, only the iron-banded mercenaries have seen combat like this. And even then, they fight other humans, not gnolls."

"There will be goblins, ogres, and trolls, too," said the man. "The goblins don't worry me much. Give them a swift kick. The ogres will be a problem."

"The trolls," the woman shook her head. "They have magic in them to dull your wits and approach you without you realizing it. And then," she brought her hand across her neck to signal how they'd slit a throat with sharp claws. Everyone shuddered.

The squirrel watched and listened. Bren wanted to ease their concerns. Polearms against the ogres. When in pain, they will strike out against anyone, including their allies. Jab with the polearms and then a quick retreat. And use fire against the trolls. They will not approach if they even see fire lit before them. The goblins were a bigger threat—of all the creatures, the goblins were intelligent. Their resourcefulness made them dangerous. These thoughts ran through Bren's mind, but the squirrel could say nothing, so Bren continued to listen.

Their captain, a gray-haired individual—not clearly masculine or feminine in presentation, a slight form, but with angular facial features on a smooth face—approached with a metal rod and poked at the fire to stir the dying embers.

"I've been thinking about this battle," the captain said, standing next to those sitting near the fire. "It's a test of who we are. Nothing more. A test. We must determine what's most essential. Is it better to be good, wise, or brave? The priests ask for goodness. The philosophers ask for wisdom. And the generals? They go on about the importance of bravery. The priests are isolated, without a care in the world. Hardly a place to test your goodness. And philosophers surround themselves with other philosophers, echoing their ideas back and forth, each pretending they thought it up. The generals are the worst. Most of them are safely at the back when we're facing down the enemy."

The squirrel climbed down the tree and crept across the dry leaves on the ground.

"Maybe the rest," said the woman with the coin necklace, "but not Bren, and certainly not Oren. That mad man would rush into a briar patch if he felt it wronged him."

"No, not Bren the *Beloved*," the captain replied bitterly and tossed the metal rod to the ground. "She'd hang her own to make a point."

Everyone paused for a moment in grim recollection.

"What is bravery?" The captain sat down, joining them. "Can it bind an injury? Can it keep your feet dry on a long march? Can it bring back the people we've lost? Bravery is nothing. It's a word. It's air. The only people who have it are the ones who have already died in this war, and to them who are now nothing, bravery is nothing."

"I disagree," said the woman. She looked around, making sure she had everyone's attention. "Bravery is everything. Hear me out. Do you know what is brave? Childbirth. And where would we be without the people willing to bring this worthless lot into the world? Eh? Being a farmer is brave. You bury your livelihood in the ground and hope that something comes from it. The life you live, the food you eat, the ale you drink, the clothes on your back—all of it is yours because someone was brave enough to bring something good into the world and share it with you."

"By your philosophy, simply waking up in the morning is a noble act," said the man sharpening his sword. "So much of that is routine, tradition, impulse, and biding our time. We call it bravery, but we've been trained to follow our captains into battle. Then, if we survive, we pat ourselves on the back and celebrate our virtue. We were brave. Ignoring the fact that a few hours previous, we were pissing our pants while feeling utterly helpless in the middle of a battlefield."

"Is it better to be good, wise, or brave?" Haim repeated his captain's question. "I think it's impossible to be good if you're not brave. It's hard to do the right thing when temptations challenge us. And it's impossible to be wise if you're not brave. Speaking the truth can be dangerous, especially when ignorant people aren't willing to listen. In the end, it all comes down to courage. If you have it, everything else is possible. If you don't, nothing matters."

When Haim finished speaking, he grabbed a stoppered jug of water, pulled the cork, and poured some water into a cup. He took a long drink. The silence lasted long and felt heavy in the air.

"Few die well that die in a battle." The man held up his

sword. He tilted it so he could look down the length of the blade, examining the edge. "May our deaths haunt the high general. The way she throws us against the enemy, I sometimes wonder if we matter at all."

The squirrel climbed back up the tree and raced across one of the limbs, jumping from one branch to the branch of another tree. Darting along these paths, the squirrel traveled to the other end of the camp. The squirrel saw two guards keeping watch. One was the son of a wealthy merchant, a fur trader from Mahynl'leth, which meant someday this guard would become a wealthy merchant. He was bold and confident, as only the children of wealth can be. His frame was awkward and lanky. His unfortunate face had ill-formed features that jutted in every direction. The other guard was the son of a farmer from Oulent, which meant one day it would be his farm, as it had been passed through their family for as long as anyone cared to recall. This guard was the physical opposite of the man standing next to him. He was strong and well-proportioned. He had a soft, innocent face, which matched his soft and innocent demeanor. These two guards had nothing in common. And as it often goes, they had become the best of friends, closer to each other than a brother. The war had brought them together. They stood away from the campfires so their eyes could adjust better to the darkness as they looked for darker forms that may threaten the camp. The squirrel worked its way down the tree to hear what they had to say.

The farmer heard the scrambling along the tree and looked up. "It's rare for a squirrel to be active at night."

"No one is getting much sleep tonight," the merchant said. "And I don't blame anyone for it. If you knew tomorrow was to be your last day, would you waste the hours in sleep? The battle will come either way. I promise you, no one is going to fall asleep in the middle of it."

"True enough. Perhaps we're keeping the squirrel awake with our chatter. This fight doesn't belong to the squirrel. I feel bad for keeping him up."

The two guards looked at each other and then laughed.

"Do you think the high general is sleeping soundly?"

The farmer considered his friend's question. "No, I don't think so. She may not fear death the way we do. But this battle will be her legacy for good or for ill. And that's enough to keep anyone awake."

"What a luxury. Here I am worried about my life. And yours, but mostly mine."

"You know what I wouldn't want to do on the night before my last day?"

"What's that?" The merchant kept his eyes focused on the darkness beyond the camp.

"Spend it talking about my high general." The farmer nudged the merchant. "I spend all day following her orders. I lose sleep having to keep guard on the eastern side *for her*—and no one's coming from this direction. At least, at the very least, my conversations can be my own."

"What do you want to talk about?"

"Marit." The farmer said her name with such tenderness.

"Her again? You made her up."

"I did not. She's as real as you. And if we survive tomorrow, I'll return home and ask her to marry me."

"She won't say no—"

"Thank you."

"—because she doesn't exist." The merchant snorted.

"And why do you think she's not real?"

"You talk about her like she's a damn unicorn. I half expect her to have a spiral horn protruding from her head the next time you describe her to me. Does she walk on air? Do rainbows follow her wherever she goes?"

"You tease too much. Marit is beautiful. The most beautiful person I've ever met."

"And here we go. Tell me about the horn coming out of her forehead."

"She's the type of beauty that strikes you so fiercely it's hard to form words. My heart beats fast. I can't breathe."

"That's not love. That's exhaustion."

"Her dark hair is always held in place by this beaded snood." The farmer put his hands to his head to pantomime the hairnet. "It makes her look like a duchess."

"Is this a tavern song? Are you about to sing a song about Marit with the beaded snood?"

"You asked me who I want to talk about, and now you give me grief for it. Do you have anyone of importance in your cynical little life?"

"I have a dog." The merchant couldn't help but smile at the thought of his pet. "She's a good breed. A wolfhound. Nice shaggy gray coat. She's a good girl. Gentle, playful. My neighbor's kids promised to take care of her while I was away. It's been years. Sometimes, when I'm lonely, I think about my dog and how much I like to go for a walk outside the city, along the river, and have her follow by my side. If the world were a fair place, dogs would outlive their masters."

"See? Not all hounds are bad." At this comment, they both laughed. The farmer patted the merchant on the back. "Let's outlive the gnolls and end this war."

. . .

Bren opened her eyes. The tent was empty.

She felt lonely, unbearably lonely. She thought of Owyn and their days at the Eloe Vale tavern. She was never alone when she had a drink in her hand. Owyn was there to raise a mug to Bren and tell her she was destined for greatness. But if she was to be great, she couldn't do it with Owyn by her side. He was a drowning man, pulling her down. When Marcus Tom told Bren to choose between being the high general's protégé or staying in Eloe Vale, it was easy to reject Owyn because, in a sense, he had given her permission. He said, "banish me." But she was the one in exile.

"Yulie," Bren called out to her cupbearer, but there was no response from outside the tent. "Yulie!" Again, silence. In that silence, she was alone with her thoughts, which she feared more than any battle.

* * *

Speck's foot rested on top of Tomas's head. Speck rolled the head back and forth with the bottom of his foot. The head was twisted around. Tomas was plainly dead. Speck observed the uncommon placement of the spine—a jumble of broken bone, penetrating outward through the skin.

"Kret, my lord, you didn't have to kill Tomas. He was an ally."

Kret was somewhere at the back of the tent. The darkness was so great, even Speck couldn't make out his form from the void. The darkness was unnatural. It shrouded Kret Bone-breaker. It followed him. Such a darkness could be crafted through spells, but Speck knew this was something different.

The darkness was his true form, and the physical body was a veil to hide something far more terrible.

Speck heard a deep, harsh voice, a voice filled with malice, speaking from the darkness.

"We don't need Tomas in his condition." Kret gave a low grunt to concede his own joke. "The supplies are good, but would've been more helpful a few months ago. The most important matter is settled. The gates will be open. The city and all its resources will be ours when we arrive. Bren doesn't have the soldiers or supplies for a siege war."

"Then we can turn our attention to hunting the treeborn fey?" Speck sounded hopeful. He did not approve of fighting this war on two fronts. "We're spread thin, sending warbands across Amon."

"Any word from the warband we sent to the Hazelef Forest?"

"Yesterday, I was able to scry and see them. The gnolls intercepted the four druids and killed all but one. She had a baby with her that drowned in the river."

"Are you certain?" The darkness unfurled through the tent as though Kret, without moving, was now face-to-face with his war mage. The darkness reminded Speck that no matter how powerful he was or would become, Kret would always be greater.

"I saw the moment reflected upon the mirror I use." Speck turned his head from the darkness. "The druid entered the river with a baby and swam to the other side without one."

"That is not the same thing as certainty."

"It's the best I can give you, my lord." Speck took an uncomfortable step back.

"Keep an eye on that region. The fey are extraordinarily

bad at living quiet, ordinary lives. If the baby isn't dead, we'll see them again." The darkness returned to the back of the tent. "Once all the warbands reconvene in Gandryll, we'll make a greater push against Aberton and the sprite grove in the middle."

Speck returned his attention to Tomas, dead on the ground. He gave the body a few half-hearted kicks. Then Kret spoke.

"Let's talk about tomorrow's battle. Have you read Pali's Discourse on Military Tactics?"

"You know I haven't read it." Speck scowled.

"There aren't many copies in existence. Most were written in an unused variation of Volir, predating the scriptoria movement in *Cora Aspru'eir* 549."

"Why don't you just make your point?" Speck, for no particular reason, gave Tomas another kick.

"He wrote that a positional weakness can be a strength—if you know your enemy will capitalize on that weakness. It allows you a chance to plan a response. This is a reduction of Pali's concept, but the intricacies are fascinating."

"And?" Speck snapped.

"You're the only one here who understands me," Kret growled. "Humor me. Lest my more primal nature take over, and I make a meal of you."

"Apologies, my lord. Continue."

"You're confident that Bren used her owl to follow you back to the camp?"

"Yes, my lord."

"I'd prefer to remain hidden, but we will use what we know. We're marching to Gandryll. And if I were Bren, I'd meet us at this gap in the forest. It will negate our size advantage. Bren will position her archers in the tree line. It only makes sense. So we will send our trolls into the forest."

"Aubec Skarsol will be ready with a fire spell, and the trolls won't engage."

"Which is why we have the magnesia powder. It's odorless and explosive. As soon as Aubec invokes fire, he'll blow up the entire forest—taking out the trolls, the archers, and hopefully himself."

A jagged grin spread across Speck's face. "You want me to spread the magnesia along the undergrowth?"

"It's already being done."

Speck's grin widened gleefully, hungrily. As a mage, he enjoyed a good explosion—even better, if a rival mage was on the receiving end. Speck jumped in the air and brought both feet down upon Tomas's head.

II

MORNING HAD COME, but the darkness held on. Swaths of red stretched across the black sky, held up by thin columns of smoke from extinguished campfires. Soldiers doused the fires with buckets of water. The hissing noises joined the songs of morning birds and the low chatter among the soldiers as they prepared for their march.

Inside the high general's tent, Bren stood with Grimni, a dwarven blacksmith. Bren knew of Grimni's reputation as a master of his craft and, months ago, she sent scouts to retrieve him for a special commission. Finally, it was ready. Bren ran her hand over the new plate armor, admiring his work.

"This armor is amazing, nearly identical to my original," Bren said as she tilted the breastplate toward the lamplight to examine it. "I'm a little sentimental about the dents from the beginning of the war. You didn't feel the need to reproduce them?"

"Thank you, general, and no, the dents must be earned," Grimni said. He wore a black leather apron and the tools of his trade on his belt. His long, thick hair was as black as his apron. Unlike most armorers, Grimni did not pull his hair into a ponytail but let it fall over his shoulders. He stroked his beard as he spoke. "I've spent a lifetime honing my skill. What you see are the fruits of that labor."

"And the belt strap here—"

"You noticed. I added an extra notch, and the buckle is different. It's narrower. This plate should fit better. Every soldier, even a general, wastes away on wartime rations. The armor needed to be adjusted. If you miss your old armor, I polished it, wrapped it, and left it near your travel sack."

"When the war is over, come to Rhyll and serve as the Northern Army's master blacksmith," Bren handed the new plate back to Grimni so he could help her don it.

Grimni gave a polite bow and began fastening the breastplate over Bren's gambeson. "I would be honored, but I must refuse. My life and my husband are in Rotwa. If Tariel had to abandon his bakery, he would never let me hear the end of it."

Bren grunted as Grimni pulled at the straps. "I understand. I'm a high general. History has proven we can be replaced. But a good marriage? That's more precious."

"No one will ever replace the Northern Light."

"But look to the *east*, the sunrise is new every morning."

"I'm sorry to break it to you, but that's the same sun."

"Are you sure?" Bren gave Grimni a nudge. She felt comfortable around Grimni in a way she hadn't felt around other people in quite some time. He lifted her spirits.

"Oh, I asked around. Everyone agrees on this one. That

fiery chariot is the same one you saw yesterday and the day before."

Bren placed her hand on Grimni's shoulder while he attached the elbow guards.

"Then promise me this: if you ever train a worthy apprentice, send them my way."

"I promise. Anything else?" Grimni patted her arm to indicate he needed the other arm so he could attach the sleeve, elbow, and gauntlet.

"Perhaps you can help me with a concern I have about today's battle."

"I'm no strategist. I can barely play chess."

"All I need is someone with a good head on their shoulders." Bren could hear the heavy footsteps of Oren approaching her tent. The man was a terror on the battlefield, but there was no stealth in him. He was inevitably checking to see what was taking her so long, even though she was still on time. It was his way. "How do I lure Kret into single combat? If I can do that, we have a chance. If not, then it's all lost."

Grimni gave a measured response.

"Don't be deceived into thinking you and Kret Bonebreaker want the same things. You want to be victorious and win the war, and thus, you think he also wants to be victorious. That's a lie."

"I don't follow."

"Winning the war would mean ending the war. And I don't think Kret wants the war to ever end." Grimni finished fastening Bren's armor and took her hand, a fatherly gesture. Bren was struck with its gentleness. "My child, facing you in single combat would be the fastest way to end this war. Why would he want that? Wherever he's going, he's going there to dig in and prolong the fight. If you want to face him in battle, you'll need to trick him into it. Think like Tian."

Tian, again. Bren looked at Grimni, stunned. Did Grimni know her thoughts? Before she could speak, Oren entered the tent. His face was red, flushed with anger.

"Bren! Your soldiers are waiting on you. It's time to go."

"Calm down, Oren. They won't start the battle without me."

Bren walked to the tent flap. She looked back at Grimni and mouthed the words, "thank you."

* * *

Lines of soldiers progressed along a narrow path in the forest. Dappled light broke through the forest canopy. The shuffling sound of the march silenced all bird and animal noises. The occasional crack of a tree branch broke the relative stillness. The wet morning smell of moss and mushrooms was sweet and peculiar.

The calvary rode their horses on the right side of the line. The riders bent over in the saddles, cramped in this tunnel-like thoroughfare. It was the most vulnerable part of their journey. If Kret ambushed them here, Bren would not have much recourse. But she also knew Kret's legion had little discipline to lie in wait for such an attack. Bren had sent scouts ahead, along with Ruth. All was clear.

Bren and Aubec rode side by side at the front—Bren on a black horse, Aubec on a buckskin horse. Oren skipped ahead. He was so large, it would be too cruel to have a horse carry him.

Oren practiced with his two-handed sword, fighting imaginary foes as he went. He was the one person who appeared to be in good spirits.

Bren looked at Aubec. They both knew this conversation was long overdue.

"Which noble families from Gandryll are you speaking to?"

"I can't tell you." And with those words, Aubec confessed to his treachery. "It'd be their death."

"You'd rather me kill all the noble families?"

"You wouldn't." Aubec said it, but he didn't sound certain.

"Yesterday, you didn't think I would hang one of my soldiers for desertion. You don't know what I'm capable of."

"They aren't plotting against you. They only want to support you, and they can't do it if you keep them at an arm's length."

Bren looked ahead as she rode. Her brow wrinkled. He didn't believe this, did he?

"That's what they told you, and you believed them." Bren sighed. "This is collusion. You've betrayed me."

"You wouldn't listen to them. I kept them informed of our situation. That's all. Nothing they couldn't have learned without me. The nobles deserve a seat at the table—"

"There's no table! It's just me making decisions." Bren raised her voice. Oren turned around to make sure Bren was okay. She waved him off.

"You reject the monarchy. Yet, you act like a monarch," Aubec said flatly.

"You don't get to make these decisions behind my back."

Bren was at a loss for words. She wanted to strangle him. Aubec didn't apologize for his betrayal or even understand he had done anything wrong. He believed the future of Amon was a return to its old greatness. He trusted the nobles. If they were allied with Kret, a real possibility, then anything Aubec shared with them, he unwittingly shared with the enemy. People had been killed for lesser crimes. Yesterday, a soldier was killed for less. And yet, as a mage, he was worth a hundred soldiers, a thousand. He evened the odds. She couldn't fight this war without Aubec. Damn him.

"When this war is over, if we survive, we'll talk more." Bren needed to end this conversation and focus on the battle ahead. "I'm sending you to Sage Hall, where you will spend the rest of your days as a teacher. Have you seen the living conditions? It's beyond squalid. Not the comfort you're used to. And their salaries? How could one afford any luxuries on such a stipend? You must do it because you love the children, but the children are all intolerable aristocrats, like yourself."

"This is my punishment. Clever. And if I refuse?"

"You're still a soldier under my command. I'm sending you to Sage Hall as a military assignment. If you refuse, I'll have you killed. You once told me that you serve the people of Amon. A noble sentiment, but who do you take orders from?"

Aubec's face twisted at the bitterness of his fate.

"I live to serve. And now, I serve to live."

Bren could see a scout farther down the path. He waved to signal all was clear. They were close to the opening in the forest that cut perpendicular to their path, providing a route from Pynne's Field to Gandryll.

"Also, if I die in battle, I want you to take over as high general."

Aubec choked on the air. He coughed and gagged from the

shock. It was not a subtle reaction. Bren had finally succeeded in catching him off guard.

"You—would offer this—to me, after I—betrayed you?" Aubec struggled to get the words out.

"Being high general is the punishment." Bren's response was quickly delivered. That pleased her. Owyn Oldcastle always had a comeback, and she wanted to be like him in that way, to wield her words like a knife. But this offer was no joking matter. "Would you use such a position to restore the monarchy?"

"I may be a descendant of Siljard, but I'm no king. My path was set a long time ago when I became a mage. This spellbook," he patted the book satchel hanging at his side, "is my kingdom. I may be a monarchist. That's my politics. That doesn't mean I want the throne for myself."

Bren noted that Aubec didn't answer her question—only stating that *he* wouldn't become king. "It'd be a shame to save Amon from Kret, only to destroy it in a civil war."

"Let's hope you can keep the peace with the nobles. A marriage perhaps?"

Bren laughed at Aubec's words. She wasn't good at peace, but she also didn't want to face Aubec as an enemy.

"End one war today. Prevent another one tomorrow," Bren muttered.

"At least we have Oren." Aubec pointed to their friend with his enormous sword, who was exuberantly hacking at pretend hounds left and right along the path.

* * *

The white barn owl circled over the open field, keeping watch for Kret's legion. Once satisfied, Bren commanded the owl to swoop down and land on her shoulder.

The soldiers gathered on the dew-covered grassy field at the bottom of a hill. The dew sparkled in the sunlight. A cold breeze cut across and whipped at Bren's exposed face. Her cheeks reddened from it. High General Bren Caius sat on her black horse and looked over the soldiers. Stretched along the path, it had seemed like there were more of them. Grouped together, the army was much smaller. The war had thinned their numbers. Bardol's death yesterday led to a few more late-night desertions. A few hundred remained? Yes, but not much more.

The soldiers stood ready for Bren Caius to issue the next command.

A lifetime later, her son, Mendal, would ask her what she had been thinking that morning before addressing the troops with the famous "sixth week of Veri'noth" speech. Bren tried to give Mendal the most honest answer. She had been asked this question throughout her life, and she mostly responded with a pithy statement about trying to remember the words Aubec had written for her. She'd then give a wry smile and change the subject. But truthfully, the entire speech came to her in a moment of inspiration. She told Mendal that, in the moment, she had been thinking of Grimni, the kind armorer who was dragged halfway across Amon, who spent weeks crafting a beautiful suit of armor. She didn't want his work to be in vain. She wanted to fight Kret and test herself against him. She wanted to survive. She wanted to send these soldiers home to their families. She wanted so many things, and it all came down to that day and that moment. Mendal gave her a contemptuous look—the child had an arsenal of such responses to anything she said—but Bren could only smile.

At Pynne's Field, the soldiers waited for Bren to speak. She addressed them with a steady voice. It was a well-rehearsed voice, the one she used to assure others that she was in charge, and they need not worry.

"You have met with your captain and know your part to play in this battle. You know where you are to be positioned and with whom. Yes?"

The soldiers nodded in unison. It amused Bren to see such a choreographed agreement.

"If you're not certain, check with your captain again. I'd rather you appear foolish than face the wrong direction when Kret and his legion arrive." The soldiers laughed. The slumped shoulders and downward cast eyes of the morning march were gone. Their attention was on their leader. From serving in High General Marcus Tom's army, Bren knew soldiers tended to follow the mood of their leaders more than their words. Marcus Tom was a fearful man—a good man, but weak. He lacked the charisma to wage war. Bren understood the theatrics of leadership. She spoke loudly with confidence—not unlike Owyn Oldcastle holding court at the tavern.

"I have one request. Kill ten. I'd task you with killing only half a hound if we were the larger party. But since we will be outnumbered, kill ten. And if you die before reaching ten, your fellow soldiers must make up the difference." More warm laughter. "Since that's not fair to them, you must live . . . and?"

Bren waited for a response. One soldier shouted in response, "Kill ten!"

Bren pointed to the soldier. "Aye, Sitrick knows his duty."

Aubec looked at Bren in surprise. She knew the soldier's

name. Aubec didn't think she bothered to know them. Bren returned his expression as though to say, "don't underestimate me."

"Kill ten," Bren continued. "If any remain, Oren will take care of the rest." Oren raised his fist in agreement, and the soldiers around him patted him on the back. The mood shifted. "If we are marked to die, I would rather do it here, today, by your side than anywhere else. And those that live, they will have the greater share of the honor. I'm happy for them to have it." The soldiers nodded again, aware of the high stakes of this battle. Gone was the memory of Bren the Beloved who unjustly executed one of their own. It had only been a day, but how quickly this cruel deed was forgotten with the right words and a charming smile. "I'm not a person who covets riches. I don't need fine clothes or estates. I spent many years drinking the cheap wine, and it got me drunk like anything from the finest vineyard. I've never dwelt on the outward things. But if it's a crime to covet honor, then I am the guiltiest person. I would not have one soldier more among our ranks if it meant I had to further share in the honor of this day. So, I say to you, do not wish for one more! We, gathered here, are enough."

Each soldier looked at the person standing next to them, holding the other in high esteem.

"If there's anyone among us who doesn't have the stomach for this fight, they can leave. I'll even give them the coin for their trip home." Bren pulled from her saddle bag a pouch of coins. She weighed it in her palm. "I would not die in that person's company if they're not willing to die with us." Bren tossed the pouch on the ground. She waited a moment, but no one reached for the coin. She then drew her sword and held it high. "Today is the start of the sixth week of Veri'noth. Verin the Traveler, his time is coming to an end. Tian's month will soon begin. To those who outlive this day and travel safely home, you will remember the sixth week of Veri'noth for the rest of your life. Every year on this week, you show your children the scars of this day and tell them the story. I fought at Pynne's Field. I killed my ten. And I would've killed ten more if Bren Caius had asked it of me."

The soldiers shouted a "huzzah!" so loudly and with such enthusiasm, it shook Bren's insides. Ruth was startled and took flight.

"I do not see a small band of soldiers. I see a mighty assemblage of siblings, siblings all." Bren was caught up in the moment. She shouted her final words. "Let no one say they are without family! Because on this day, you are my family! My kin! There will be many folk in Amon who will wish they had been here on this day to test their courage, to test their worth, and to fight by our side on this fateful day!"

Bren's voice cracked when she shouted the last word. She cringed at the shrillness of her voice. She had always tried to avoid such oratory flaws, but no one noticed or cared.

The soldiers shouted, "For victory! For Amon! For Bren!"

The shouts continued as the soldiers rushed to their positions on the field and beyond. As each one passed, they bowed their heads to Bren in reverence. Bren reached down from where she sat on her mount and touched their helmets, a blessing of sorts.

A woman marched with her troops, a pike resting on her shoulder. She wore a maroon hooded cloak over her brigandine armor. Bren called out to her.

"Tamsin! Come here!"

Tamsin walked to Bren and looked up at her, squinting as though she were looking at the sun. "General?"

Bren dismounted from her saddle and looked Tamsin over. They were the same height, similar build.

"Tamsin, tell your captain you will not be with the pikes at the vanguard. I need you for something else."

Tamsin accepted this new charge without hesitation. She handed her pike to another soldier walking by. Tamsin held her hands out to signal she was ready for anything. "General, did I get a promotion?"

* * *

Oren was with the vanguard. The soldiers formed a line three deep across the narrow field. They stood at the bottom of a hill. On either side was densely wooded forest. The soldiers' pikes were angled upward, the ends braced against the ground. Oren held up his two-handed sword, assessing its size, which was nearly as long as the pikes.

"Kret's legion will make a lot of noise," Oren addressed the soldiers to the left and to the right. "They want to show us we're outnumbered. But we already know that. Let them huff and puff and stomp around. We're not going anywhere. They'll send the ogres at us first. They'll run at you, and it's a scary sight. I've never known anyone who hasn't second guessed their life choices at that moment. It takes real courage to stand firm, but it's the best thing to do. Let the pikes do their job. When they pierce the ogre's thick hide, it'll enrage the ogre and they'll attack anyone around them—including each other. Back up twenty paces, at least. Wait for them to finish their tantrum, and then as a single unit, move up again. Understand?"

"Yes, sir," the soldiers responded as one.

Oren snarled in a self-satisfied manner. "I like this group. We'll have some fun—"

A blast of horns interrupted from the other side of the ridge. The low rumble of the approaching horde rolled down the hill. Bren's owl circled over the ridge. Bren could be heard farther back shouting to her soldiers that Kret was nearby. That was plain to everyone. A dark line of monstrous warriors emerged over the ridge. More kept coming until they were a writhing mass consuming the top of the hill. They blew bukkehorns and beat on drums. The incessant growls and baying of the gnolls was even louder. Bren had said to kill ten, but it appeared as though even five times that would not be enough. The battle was futile, and it hadn't even begun.

"Courage, friends. Courage," Oren said, sensing the unease of the soldiers. "You're doing fine. This battle must be fought to be decided. I'm not going to concede to their drums and horns and howling." Then, as if the other side hung on Oren's word, the drumming stopped. "Now come the ogres."

As Oren predicted, Kret's army split in the middle, and a pack of ogres stormed out from the opening. They bounded down the hill with such speed some of them lost their footing and tumbled toward the soldiers. There were more ogres than Oren had anticipated. He counted twelve. Oren gripped his sword tighter and resisted the urge to run out to meet them.

The ogres were nearly upon the vanguard. Their approach thundered like titans breaking through the earth, like the world ending. The tumult shook Oren's insides. He shouted

"Courage! Hold!" But he doubted the others could even hear him.

The ogres crashed into the wall of soldiers, scattering them in every direction. They were flung in the air as the ogres flailed about with their thick arms and boulder-sized fists. The ogres had pikes sticking in them like the needles of a pincushion. The pain sent the ogres into a blind rage, screaming and swinging wildly. Some fought each other. And others ran back up the hill toward the gnolls and goblins. The vanguard rushed back several paces as Oren had instructed. Not all of them made it. One stray hit from an ogre was enough to shatter a person's bones and splatter their insides across the field.

Oren ran his sword through the neck of an ogre. He had to push it through with great effort. Once it penetrated the other side, the wide blade nearly decapitated the ogre. The creature's head flopped over, blood pouring from the neck wound and his mouth. Oren roared in triumph and yanked the sword free. The ogre collapsed to the ground.

The remaining ogres clustered at the bottom of the hill in their berserk state, striking at each other and forming a wall between Oren and the other soldiers. Oren had no choice but to fight his way through. He took a cautious step forward, crouching low to the ground. He took another step and then jabbed his sword into an ogre's calf tendons. The ogre fell over, and another ogre jumped on him, pummeling with his fists. Oren snuck past. An ogre stepped in front of Oren and roared. Oren swung his sword, but the ogre grabbed the blade, unfazed as the sword cut into his hand. The blood coated the steel blade. The ogre yanked the sword from Oren and flung it. Oren ran toward where his sword had landed, but the ogre flanked him before he could retrieve the weapon. Oren balled his fists and bared his teeth. He had fought well, and he would die with honor.

Before the ogre could charge, he grimaced. Confusion spread across his face. And then, he was dead. Several pikes were lodged deep into his back. The vanguard had returned to the original line to defend their commander.

Most of the ogres were wounded from their reckless advance. The vanguard was able to finish them off, but the victory was costly. The front lines were depleted by half. Not enough of the vanguard remained to block the way unless they spread farther apart. Dead soldiers were scattered across the field, up along the hillside. The injured soldiers who survived would not live much longer. They moaned for help, for family in distant cities, and for someone to stop the pain. Other soldiers knelt by their side, holding their hand, and giving them false promises of what they would do after the war. They would remind them of how brave they were. This irregular chorus of agonized cries was a worse sound than the thunder of war. It occupied the silence before the next wave of battle, and it reminded the soldiers that the pain of death diminished everyone. It would turn the boldest warrior into a terrified child. The soldiers did not want to hear the cries because their truth was uncomfortable. The crying shattered all notions of war as a proud and glorious thing. They wanted to believe they were fighting for Amon, for their families—and they were— but in these moments, they were only fighting to stay alive and unbroken. They did not want to be one of the scared, crying soldiers who didn't get the benefit of a quick death.

Oren, however, was intrigued by the agony. He saw the pain as a transcendent experience. They were closer to the unspeakable, unknowable whole of creation, and for Oren, that was not something to be ashamed of. He watched with passive curiosity. As a youth, he had often visited the butcher in his home village. He would look into the eyes of the livestock as their throats were cut and they bled out. There was fear, pain, confusion. All the normal responses. They struggled against the harness before going still. If it made Oren a monster to be fascinated by death, then he was a monster. He didn't mind.

Ruth flew overhead in a wide double arc. This signal from Bren let the infantry know to form a shield wall and prepare for the onslaught.

Aubec folded his red cape and placed it in his bag next to the spellbook, which was stored in a dried calf's bladder. Aubec did not want the red cape to catch the attention of Kret's legion as he and the archers crept through the dense forest alongside the field. The archers moved into place, spread out along the inclined tree line. Each one hid, sitting with their back against a tree for greater cover. They had emptied their quivers, sticking the arrows into the ground so they could quickly grab and nock new arrows. Aubec watched through the brush as gnolls and goblins marched past them, down the hill. The gnolls formed a shield wall and walked in step. They were more beast than human, but in moments like this, Aubec was amazed at how the pack mentality kept them operating as one unit. They would happily abandon the shield wall once they received the order from Kret—but for now, they were like any other disciplined army.

Aubec looked for Speck but could not find him. Once the two infantries clashed, the plan was for the archers to rain their arrows upon the exposed force. Aubec would then contain the enemy from any retreat or attempt at cover. He also needed to negate anything Speck had planned.

It would be a tiring battle. Aubec wasn't used to casting so much during a single conflict. In this regard, Speck was the stronger war mage, able to endure more castings. But if Bren's plan worked, it would all be over soon, with either Bren or Kret victorious.

Aubec wanted Bren to win. Naturally. It went without saying. She was his friend, and she was the best person to lead Amon. Aubec believed that. He also knew he'd be punished as a traitor after this was all over. However, if Bren lost, he'd be celebrated as a hero for helping the nobles negotiate with Kret. Whatever the outcome, Aubec would lose.

Ravi was the captain of the archers on this side of the forest. Another group of archers were on the other side. Ravi crawled to Aubec and held up his hand. Ravi's fingers were coated with white powder.

"This powder is scattered along the ground. The other archers have noticed it, too. It itches and burns a little when you touch it."

"Then don't touch it?" Aubec whispered at him. They were seconds away from ambushing the enemy, and Ravi was asking for an alchemy lesson. "Some blighted plants will have a powdery mildew on them."

"That is not this," Ravi hissed at him. Aubec looked again. The powder was something different. Aubec got a sick feeling in his stomach.

"Command your archers." Aubec jumped from his hiding place, all stealth forgotten. If he was correct, then Speck knew he'd be here, which meant none of them were safe. "Strike now. I'll worry about the powder."

Aubec reached in his bag for the cape. He needed to get out of the forest to find Speck. And he wasn't going to confront his old friend without his cape.

The gnolls and goblin came down the hill with their weapons drawn and their shields in front of them. It was a common misconception that whoever had the high ground was automatically at an advantage. Bren could think of three examples in her studies of military history—two in Amon, one in Lunthal—where the high ground was more of a hindrance. Two examples involved a mountain siege where the army at the top couldn't get access to supplies or reinforcements. The example from Lunthal was applicable to this battle. An elven army was trapped on a narrow pass and ambushed on both sides—a strategic retreat made matters worse as soldiers trampled over each other to get back. That's what Bren was hoping for here.

The two shield walls collided. Hungry gnolls growled and snapped, separated from their foes, mere inches away. The soldiers grunted as they leaned in, trying to push back the opposing force.

When they first gathered at the bottom of the hill, the soldiers had been told to dig narrow divots into the earth to create footholds for better leverage. It worked. Despite being outnumbered, despite the raw strength of the other side, Bren's army did not yield.

Swords, spears, and axes still found their way through the gaps in the shield wall. One soldier was jabbed in the eye with a spear tip. The blood rushed out. He screamed. Other soldiers covered the space he created. An axe chopped at another soldier's arm, cutting it off. Blood sprayed everyone around. Soldiers behind this man dragged him away from the front line. They called for a barber surgeon to cauterize and bind the wound. A sword pierced another soldier's side. She gritted her teeth and pressed her shield harder against the opposing side. She kept shouting "I'm good" as other soldiers asked if she needed to move to the back. The sword slid in deeper. "I'm good. I'm good. I'm good." The soldier died where she stood. But the Northern Army's line held.

The soldiers retaliated with swords, spears, axes, and polearms of their own. They thrust through the openings until they heard a yelp of pain and the resistance of thick hide against sharp blade. The goal was not to push Kret's legion back, if it was even possible. They were to hold them in place, to keep them here until the archers fired. The seconds dragged on.

The gnolls and goblins kept approaching, pressing upon their shieldbearers and making it harder for them to stand. More and more of Kret's legion crowded in.

Bren closed her eyes and compelled Ruth, flying above the battle, to give the signal for the archers. Ruth swooped low and then flew straight up. The snaps of bow strings could be heard throughout the forest. From the tree line on both sides, arrows whistled through the air. The many arrows formed a dark mist of death. Each arrow, a loud thunk connecting with their fleshy target. This was the archer's melody.

Not a single gnoll or goblin had their shields ready. They fell to the ground. The surviving infantry tried their best to retreat, but they tripped over the bodies. More creatures stepped upon them as they moved back. Again, the arrows came from the forest and more bodies fell.

Bren did not want to allow herself a moment to hope, but she saw how the archers obliterated the hounds' shield wall. Victory was possible. She drew her sword and moved forward.

Aubec and the archers were alone in the forest. And then the trolls arrived.

Aubec did not see them approach. They glided in among the archers. Their gaunt, towering presence was dizzying. All sense of time was gone. Aubec knew he was in danger. The archers around him were being cut down where they stood. Necks slashed open from long, pointed fingers. No one made the effort to run or scream. Aubec couldn't find the will to move. He was lost in a dreamlike sense of paralysis. What was he supposed to do? Fire. Yes, fire. The trolls did not like fire.

A troll raised his hand to strike at Aubec. The war mage found himself casting a spell. This knowledge came instinctively. Even his muddled consciousness could not prevent him from casting.

The barrage of arrows ceased. The infantry looked around, confused. Why did the archers stop? The ranged attacks had thinned out the front lines of Kret's legion. Chaos reigned as the gnolls and goblins stumbled over the fallen. Survivors along the front attempted to move back while those in the back were moved to the front. It created space between the well-formed shield wall of the Northern Army and the broken wall of the hounds. The soldiers had to resist the urge to pursue the retreating enemy. There were scattered shouts of "hold."

Oren did not listen. He moved past the shields and struck down any hound within range of him, shouting and laughing the whole while, wading through a river of the dead, urging others to come play.

Further back, upon her black horse, a high general shouted commands.

Aubec finished casting his spell as the troll was about to bring down a clawed hand across his neck, or perhaps the troll already had. The haze of the troll's presence made it hard to tell. Aubec was still alive, so he had to assume the troll wasn't fast enough. The fire spread up the troll's body. Its face—grayish skin stretched over a distorted skull—twisted in agony, a high-pitched scream like a rock scratching across glass. The troll lit up and then burst into nothing. With the troll gone, the fog lifted, and full awareness returned to him. The archers stood motionless throughout the forest, the blank expressions of scarecrow mannequins. Trolls cut their throats and gutted them. Ravi stood next to Aubec. All he could say was a simple prayer: "Gods protect us."

The embers from the immolated troll floated to the ground, igniting the white powder on the ground. A hissing, fizzing noise shot throughout the forest as the powder reacted to the fire. Then, a rushing whoosh as though the air had suddenly been warmed and expanded. Aubec felt a crackling heat across his face.

. . .

The archers from the south forest had stopped firing, but arrows came from the north sporadically. A pack of gnolls held up their shields and moved against those active archers. Several infantry soldiers broke from the shield wall to stop the gnolls—including Oren and the woman with a maroon hooded cloak. The clear lines of ally and enemy disintegrated.

All the soldiers turned when they heard the whooshing noise. The south forest exploded in a burst of flames, sending bits of tree and earth flying. The force of the blast knocked everyone over. The heat sizzled at hair and skin. The fire rolled higher into the sky. Plumes of black smoke followed.

The forest was gone, lost in an inferno. Everything burned. The trees within this hell snapped and fell against each other. No other sounds, no screaming or panicked calls for help, could be heard. The devastation was sudden and complete. Smoke billowed as though the world were on fire.

"Aubec, what did you cast?" Oren marveled as he got to his feet. As though swatting a bothersome fly, he brought his sword down on the skull of a combatant who was slower to recover. The fight resumed.

Kret stood at the top of the hill. He watched over the battle. Speck was by his side like a faithful pet. The fire raged on the south end. Several gnolls split from the main infantry force to weed out the remaining archers on the other side of the forest. Tactically, it made sense, but it further weakened the middle of the field. Far beyond the fight was the high general in shining plate armor on her black horse with the rest of the calvary. She shouted commands.

"It's unlike Bren to stay away from the fighting," Speck said.

"It's sensible," Kret mused. "If we win this battle, she'll need an easy retreat so she can recruit more soldiers." Kret rubbed his chin as he considered Bren's options. "But her infantry's got some fight in them. If we lose more of our lot, she'll send in the calvary to further the advantage. She's hoping for a chance to face me in single combat. She wants to force my hand."

"Will you fight her?"

Kret chuckled at the thought. "Single combat is a ridiculous notion. Would I win? Most likely. But fortune is fickle. Why risk the entire war on one fight? I don't need to beat her. We just need to get past her. Even if a fraction of our legion remains, we have enough warbands scattered through Amon. We can call them to Gandryll. We'd have enough to continue the war. Still," Kret's dark eyes narrowed as he tried to get a better look at the woman on the black horse, "I do not like to lose."

Kret grabbed Speck by the neck. "Speck, you've been idle." The goblin gulped in surprise. Kret tossed him into the air, down the hill. "Even our odds."

While in the air, Speck exhaled luminous smoke, a spell. He disappeared and popped into a space behind a cluster of Bren's soldiers. He looked with a sour expression at Kret on the hilltop, and then he held his hands up, palms out. A shockwave boomed from the goblin, scattering the soldiers, breaking them. None of the fallen soldiers got back to their feet.

A soldier saw Speck and shouted, "War mage!" The other soldiers turned their attention to him. They slashed at the goblin with their swords, but it was no use. He blinked away from every attack, appearing nearby, but always out of range. Speck would place a hand on the chest of a soldier, and the soldier's chest would cave in with another smaller burst of force. Ribs and sternum cracked and snapped. The soldier vomited blood and fell to the ground. The dead lay scattered behind Speck as he moved through the infantry.

The gnolls trekked through the forest toward the archers.

These archers remembered Ilden and the battle in the tulip fields. They remembered the moment when the gnolls closed in on them and charged. It felt like they were cursed to relive that moment.

Like at Ilden, the gnolls were spaced far apart as the archers fired. The forest itself acted as a shield. The arrows were more likely to hit the trunk of a tree than a gnoll.

The archers remembered Sergeant Leylan running out to meet the gnolls by herself, being surrounded and torn apart for her courage. They could not let it happen again.

Haim had assumed command after Leylan. If he were ever going to make a name for himself, this might be the last opportunity.

He looked around, searching for some advantage.

"I need twenty of our best archers boosted into the trees," Haim shouted. "Don't take long to figure this out. Two others help them to the highest limb they can reach."

The archers looked at each other, confused. A red frustration flared across Haim's cheeks. "Now! Do it now! *Sah'le vuk!*"

The archers scrambled to help each other up the trees. The gnolls were getting closer. Once the twenty archers were in the trees, their bows nocked and ready, the remaining soldiers on the ground looked to Haim for leadership. "What next?" asked a nervous soldier.

"Drop your bows," Haim commanded as he tightened the strap of his helmet. "Draw your swords. Hold your shields high. We're luring them into this area here. We'll fight them, while our companions rain arrows from above."

"What if we get hit by a stray arrow?" The nervous one asked.

"Let's hope the archers take clean shots. But I would say the bigger threat is before us." Haim pointed to the gnolls who were running at them. "It may not seem like it, but our numbers are even. You don't even need to strike the killing blow. Just keep them in place and let the archers above us do the work."

The soldiers stood their ground. Not one of them ran away.

Haim was the first to fall. A gnoll leapt at him with jaws open wide. The gnoll's teeth snuck deep into Haim's neck. Once the gnoll had clamped on, he shook his victim viciously until the neck broke. An arrow sunk into the back of the gnoll's head and out the other side. The dead fell together. Haim's kettle helmet rolled and bounced along the wet, mossy ground.

The fight did not last long. The gnolls came at the soldiers with an unmatched ferocity. Some soldiers were able to strike down a gnoll or two, but the archers in the trees did most of the work. No one on the ground—gnoll or human—was left standing in the end.

The archers climbed down the trees, each looking to the other for guidance. They knew if they hadn't been assigned to their perch, they would be among the dead. They had survived, not because they were more deserving—but because they were lucky. And war was like that.

"We need to return to the tree line and continue firing upon the hounds," one archer said in a thin voice, shaken by the death surrounding him. "The others need us."

Another archer walked away, deeper into the forest. "I can't. I've seen enough death today. I can't do it."

He heard a voice behind him. "We will shoot you down right now if you take another step."

The remaining archers had their bows drawn and pointed at him. Maybe one or two wouldn't have the courage to kill a friend, but not all of them.

"Fine." He walked back and retrieved the arrows from the fallen hounds. "They need us. But when a gnoll has his filthy spear shoved through your heart, I hope you remember we could've lived."

Speck pruned the dense battlefield. His spellcraft was one of evasion and devastation. He could avoid attacks and immobilize large areas of the field. Mages were rare. Mages willing to study the necessary combat spells were even rarer. But if an army had a war mage, they could decide the outcome of any battle. And no general would ever take to the field without a strategy against them. Speck snickered as he blinked in and out of the masses, killing every soldier with a word and a touch. Speck appeared behind one soldier. He was a large man with kind features. He fought with determination, but he had no idea the goblin was about to cast another close-range shockwave and implode his head.

Speck spoke his words and breathed life into the spell, but

it stopped short. The magic failed. Speck felt his lungs squeeze and burn. Someone had cast a spell to block his own. Speck narrowed his eyes and looked into the raging forest fire. A shadowy form appeared. Aubec Skarsol stumbled out of the inferno.

Aubec had his cape wrapped around him. The cape was burning, which made Aubec look like an elemental spirit shrouded in flame. He threw his cape to the ground. Aubec's skin was glossy, reddened, and raw from the fire. He was in agony, but he was still standing. He coughed and winced. Then Aubec looked at Speck with a hateful glare. Aubec disappeared with a wave of his hands.

In a flash, Aubec reappeared next to the goblin. The two war mages used this spell as a dance, jumping short distances to avoid each other and gain an advantageous position over their rival. Around they went until they had both exhausted this approach.

Speck tried to breathe another spell, but Aubec, with an ancient word of power, was able to cancel the spell. Then Aubec tried the same and Speck canceled his spell.

All the while, the larger battle raged around them. The arrows from the north forest resumed, taking down more gnolls and goblins.

Aubec pushed Speck backward with the heel of his boot and spoke a different spell into existence. Smoke encircled Speck and then erupted in flames. The goblin howled.

Speck summoned a gust of wind, which blew out the flames and knocked Aubec into the mud. Earlier, the field had been pristine with tall green grass, but the battle had torn up the soft earth as the soldiers continued to fight. Speck also dropped, placing his palms upon the ground. A shockwave rippled toward Aubec, jolting him with the force. He grunted, trying to conceal his pain.

Aubec looked around, but Speck was nowhere to be seen.

Speck dropped from the sky onto Aubec. Before landing, Speck conjured a translucent disk, which he stood upon, adding greater weight onto Aubec. The hit drove Aubec down again. The disk disappeared. Aubec tackled Speck. No spells this time. The two war mages rolled around, each trying to strangle the other.

From his prone position, Aubec cast a protective wall of force that boosted Speck into the air. Aubec whispered something and sent the message out. It moved like a wave of glowing mist to the north forest. Aubec was speaking with others. Speck was confused by this seemingly harmless spell. Then Speck realized how vulnerable he was in the open, several feet above everything and everyone else. Arrows shot out from the tree line at Speck. He was able to dodge most of them with the use of his blink spell, but one arrow pierced his hand. He gasped at the injury, looking at it in disbelief.

A mage needed many things to cast spells—beyond mental focus—air in their lungs, the ability to vocalize sounds, and their hands to form the necessary gestures. The arrow, which had gone through the back of his hand and out through his palm, eliminated any ability to cast spells.

Speck leapt off the wall of force and hurried up the hill back to Kret Bonebreaker. The arrows continued to fly. Speck grabbed a shield from a dead soldier and used it to protect himself as he retreated. Aubec was too exhausted to pursue. All his spells had been spent. He couldn't cast any more for some time. If the archers had missed, Aubec wouldn't have been able to defend against Speck's magic.

Aubec rolled to his side. Everything hurt. He needed the healing salves his alchemist mother had concocted and gifted to him. It would stop the pain and keep the burns from scarring. He had kept a stash back at the camp. It would be some time before they would return. Aubec would have to endure the pain until then. He screamed as he got back to his feet.

Oren dashed to Aubec, sword dragging behind him. Oren moved to put his arm around Aubec to help him up, but thought better of touching the wounded mage.

"Thank the named gods for your protective spells. I saw the explosion in the forest, and I thought for sure you had died."

"I didn't cast a protective spell. I had just cast the fire spell, which triggered the magnesia, I'm assuming. I wasn't ready. I wasn't thinking straight. Ravi threw himself on me, shielding me from the explosion. The blast tore Ravi apart, but he saved me."

"How did you make it out?"

Aubec pointed to his cape on the ground near the edge of the burning forest. "My mother created an oil with special warding properties. I applied it to the cloth months ago. It kept the flames at bay." Aubec did not fight the tears as he thought about the sacrifices and the gifts that had kept him alive. The tears stung as they ran in rivulets down his burned face.

A batch of infantry soldiers split off from the battle and moved up the hill toward Kret Bonebreaker. Kret bared his thick canine teeth and readied his double-bit battle axe. He swung the axe in one wide circle over his head, making a whooshing sound.

"You've got some fight in you," Kret spoke in his deep

rumbling voice. "I'll say that. But it's time to end this. Gandryll awaits."

The woman with the maroon cloak broke from the group and rushed ahead to face Kret. She had the hood drawn low to conceal the top portion of her face. A few blonde strands of hair drifted out from under the hood. She held out her long sword and positioned her shield to protect her torso.

"Have at it then," Kret said as he swung his mighty axe at the foolish warrior. "You're the first."

Kret's axe had the force of a falling redwood, but it was stopped abruptly with the woman's sword, which she held in one hand. The sword and her arm were glowing a shimmering blue.

The soldier pulled back the hood to reveal her face. It was Bren Caius.

"A steady journey, Kret."

Kret looked from Bren to the other woman in plate armor mounted on Bren's horse. She waited with the calvary in the back. This other woman was a convincing double, especially from a distance.

"I smelled you," Kret grumbled. "I assumed the breeze carried it to me, but here you are."

"Your legion isn't faring well." Bren pushed with her sword to move the axe away. "You said it yourself. 'Time to end this.'" Bren pointed her sword at Kret. "I challenge you to single combat. To the death. The winner gains all the spoils of war. No treaties. No clemency."

Kret laughed.

"Why would either side honor that agreement? If you die, your soldiers will still fight. They value their lives. It's a natural impulse. And if I die, you'll have an even bigger problem controlling my hounds. They won't surrender."

"Your legion will scatter. I can spend the next few years chasing down whoever remains. But here's why you'll agree to single combat: You won't get to Gandryll unless you go through me."

"And the disguise? The trickery?"

"I've found that when I get close, the impulse to fight me is very strong. I have that effect."

"Strange. People want to run from me. Not you."

"You have me." Bren beat at her chest, daring Kret to strike first.

As Bren and Kret spoke, the fighting between the two sides died down and disentangled. Bren's soldiers approached behind her, while Kret's soldiers regrouped behind him. The hounds still outnumbered the Northern Army, but not as much as before.

The fires raged from the south. The smoke drifted across the field and blotted out much of the sky, creating an orange haze. Silver ash and red embers rained down.

Kret looked as though he were about to say something, but instead, he shrugged his resignation. Kret attacked with his axe in a snap of three lightning-quick strikes. Bren blocked the first attempt with her shield and the last two with her sword. The shield cracked from the hit. The high pitch of steel scoring against steel rang out. Blue light rippled across Bren's body like a static spark. The hits were so quick, the soldiers all stepped back, frightened by Kret's speed and strength. Each wondered how anyone could be fast enough to even see these attacks coming, let alone stop them.

Kret initiated another series of swings, with Bren blocking

each one, blue light flashing. Now Bren moved in with her attacks. Kret was able to catch Bren's blade between the head and handle of his axe, trapping it there. Bren pulled to free her sword, but Kret moved forward and head-butted her. She fell back, but not completely, as she was still holding onto her sword. She planted her back foot and moved toward Kret with her shield, pushing both axe and sword tip at Kret's chest. He pushed her aside, dislodging the two weapons from each other. Blood streamed from Kret's chest, a dark line against thick fur. Likewise, blood trickled down Bren's forehead.

Both injured. Neither noticed.

The two didn't say a word. They glared at each other with seething hate. All the pain, all the anger, she channeled at Kret. He became the embodiment of everything taken from her life. She wanted to see Owyn Oldcastle's smile one more time. She wanted to buy a round for everyone at the tavern, to sing songs, to laugh and dance. But those days were gone. Violence was all that remained. Kret was all that remained. These past few years of war had become her life, and she wanted to see it all end.

Bren had grown up during the plague years. As some of her earliest memories, she recalled gaping mouths, the sick and the dead covered in flies, and the sick smells that floated through Eloe Vale, forcing her family to abandon their home and move into the wilds for a time. These brief visions reminded Bren of the famines that spread through Amon during the war. The gnolls would burn fields and disrupt the trade routes. They would wipe out farming villages. So, when the parents holding their starving children screamed at Bren, "Why can't we buy any food? We have the coin." Bren knew the food was gone because of Kret. He was the author of so much suffering. He was the plague, and he only wanted it to continue. Everything was in delicate balance, and Kret knocked over the scales with a swipe of his hand.

Bren screamed as she ran once more at Kret. Each swing was parried. Each parry was met with a response and another attack. When actors would recreate this fight on the stage, they would choreograph a beautiful display of fencing—filled with spins and flips, rolls, and high leaps. They would save their best moves for this final fight. But that was not what happened in the actual fight. Bren and Kret chopped at each other, inelegantly trying to take the other's head off, but neither could land the finishing blow. Neither could surprise the other. It became more a battle of endurance than skill. One had to outlast the other.

Bren jumped back, barely out of the axe's range. From the swing, she could feel a slight gust of air against her cheek. She was tiring, and it would only be a matter of time before she couldn't move fast enough—whereas Kret looked even stronger and more powerful than before. It didn't seem possible. The two warriors circled each other. Kret bayed, hackles raised on his back, an instinctive response. Bren shook with blood rage.

Kret jumped high into the air. Having both feet off the ground was usually a terrible decision for any fighter, but Kret had complete control and awareness over his space. He was a whirling blur of destruction. He shot to the ground faster than Bren expected. Bren brought up her cracked shield for protection. Kret's axe split the shield in two and drove Bren onto her back. The axe stopped short of slicing into Bren Caius. The iron banding, which fortified the back of the shield, saved her. But the shield was now worthless. Bren threw it aside. She kicked up to her feet in a single graceful move. Kret was already on her. Too close to swing the axe—instead, he jabbed with it, hitting Bren's breastplate with the axe head. The plate did not dent, but it knocked the wind out of Bren. Kret jabbed again to move her back and create space. At this point, Kret was getting everything he wanted in this fight. He swung again. Bren tried to block, but it merely softened his strike as it connected with her shoulder. Bren gasped from the pain. Kret moved his axe forward and then racked it back, hooking her bruised shoulder with the bottom of the axe blade. The strike spun Bren around. Her shoulder burned in agony.

She moved back another few steps to collect herself, but Kret was relentless—swinging again and again as Bren countered the attacks with her sword. Blue light pulsed with each strike.

Bren felt lightheaded.

She stumbled, then regained her footing.

The ghastly looks from the soldiers. Owyn Oldcastle—or was it Oren—shook his head. Concerned. Disappointed. Bren could hear the singing of tavern songs in the distance.

Time to go home.

The smoke from the forest fire swirled above her. It formed a circle like the gaping mouth of a dead man. Embers like flies.

In her delirium, Bren heard a soft voice, Hild whispering in her ear, a single word. *Cerneboch*. She did not know what "Cerneboch" meant, but the name was important.

Kret.

Ancient Beast.

The Devouring Spirit.

There was no defeating him.

"Aye, a clear path to your mother's bed!" Old Owyn had once said.

"I can't entertain like I once did."

Breathe deep.

"Don't stoop to be the queen."

Keep fighting.

"Caius means joy."

Focus on the fight.

"Make me an Oldcastle."

Focus on the fight. Damn it.

The world sped up again. Axe head pounded against sword blade—clang, clang, clang, clang—a thundering reminiscent of the armorer at his anvil. Bren once again deflected each attack. She wasn't thinking. It was all intuition, a natural gut feeling, a gift from the gods. Kret's eyes were wide with surprise. He had expected to make the killing blow, but no longer.

Bren stabbed with her sword, feeling a renewed speed. The sword pierced through Kret's arm and into his side. Bren pulled the sword back, and the black blood sprayed from the wound. Where it landed on Bren's skin, it burned.

Bren shouted, "Shield!"

One soldier tossed his shield to the high general. She caught it just in time to use it to block another hit from Kret's axe. The hit sent her flying backward. She rolled along the ground and back to her feet—her sword leveled at her foe.

The two engaged in a series of strikes, parries, and ripostes, feints and lunges, so fast, so deadly in their accuracy. Neither one held anything back. Neither yielding an inch to the other.

The two clashed, axe blade against sword blade, pushing against each other. The axe was at Bren's throat. The sword pointed downward. Droplets of sweat and blood covered Bren's face. Her eyes began to roll in the back of her head. She gritted her teeth, determined to stay conscious.

"Yield!" Kret barked.

"I can't." Bren spoke in a weak and trembling voice.

Her shield rattled to the ground. In a flash of blue light, Bren placed both hands on the pommel of the sword and pushed it down, thrusting the sword into Kret's foot. She then leaned in with her uninjured shoulder, shoving Kret over. He landed on his back. Bren did not have a second to spare. She took her sword and deftly climbed the beast. Bren drove her sword through Kret's chest. Blood spouted from the mortal wound. Bren screamed as Kret's blood boiled on her exposed flesh. Kret gasped in surprise. His mouth twisted into a toothy smile, and then he died. His body went limp. Bren fell to the ground from exhaustion.

Bren lost consciousness for a moment. She woke in a confused state. Her soldiers rushed past her. Were they running away? Did they lose the battle? But then she noticed they were charging after the hounds. Kret's legion was retreating. They scattered in all directions, as Bren had predicted.

Oren's face appeared directly over Bren, and she flinched at his presence.

"Bren, get up! You killed Kret Bonebreaker. The war is over."

Bren rested her aching head upon the earth. She could hear it humming beneath her. "Did I now? Well, that's lovely." Bren groaned. "That's lovely. Well done."

* * *

The soldiers carried Bren back to her tent. The lamps were lit. Incense burned. She drifted in and out of consciousness all day. The battle was early in the morning, but when Bren rolled over, she noticed the night sky through the thin slit of the tied door flap.

She remembered at one point in the day the pain had been unbearable. She was burning with fever from her injuries. Hild and several other people had held her down as they wrapped her wounds and applied ointment. She called for druids and their healing magic, but there were no druids conscripted in her army. For all she knew, there were no druids anywhere in Amon. She called for an alchemist, but they had already plied their trade, and the pain persisted. She had called for Aubec, but he was nowhere to be found. Oftentimes, after battles, he retreated to study his book. Then a fitful sleep came over her.

Now it was night, and Bren was wide awake.

Ruth was on her perch, gnawing at a field mouse she had captured earlier. Ruth tore at the mouse. The sound was like a washcloth being ripped in two.

Hild sat nearby, leaning against a post and resting her eyes.

Yulie stood farther back. She held a flagon of wine, awaiting Bren's next command.

Bren rolled in the other direction. She almost jumped off the cot. She cursed. Her heart raced. Someone, probably Oren, thought hauling Kret's body into the tent was a good idea.

"It's unsettling, isn't it?" Hild commented, eyes still closed.

Kret was large. His still and stinking body occupied the entire length of the tent. His presence felt more real inside the tent. Bren gaped at his size and his taut muscles. How was she able to survive a hit from him without being torn in two? She looked at the wound in his chest where she had driven her sword. The sword had been removed, cleaned, polished even, and placed against a chair on the other side of the tent. The sword would be largely ceremonial now. The sword that had killed Kret Bonebreaker. The wound was smaller than she remembered. But then again, the fight was a blur. She couldn't recall many details. The poets would have to fill in the rest.

Next to the body was an arcane crate made from walnut, painted black with a series of runic patterns carved along the lid. No doubt this was Aubec's contribution. They would need proof the great evil was dead and gone, and Aubec wouldn't want anyone to steal the remains.

"Yulie, my throat is parched." Bren waved her over. "Bring me some wine."

The girl walked over. Bren heard the sounds of the celebration outside her tent. The sounds were there when she first woke, but she didn't discern them until now. The soldiers were drinking. Bren heard the clanking of copper cups in wassail toasts paired with hearty cheers. She heard the singing of songs and merrymaking. Bren thought she could hear the stomping of feet. A dance. She heard one soldier bragging about his ten kills. She heard another's drunken rambling about how he always wanted to be an archer and when he returned home, he'd learn how to use a longbow, and then he'd teach his children. Bren thought about reaching out with her second sight to see the celebration but decided against it. The joyous sounds were enough.

Yulie poured the wine. Bren held up two fingers, indicating she wanted a second glass. Yulie obliged and then moved back to where she was before. She did not turn her back to Kret.

"He can't hurt you anymore," Bren murmured as much to herself as to Yulie.

"I still don't like seeing him."

Bren took a long drink of her wine.

"Was it Oren's idea to leave him in here like some trophy?"

"It was," Yulie and Hild answered in unison.

Bren sat on the edge of the cot, facing Kret's body. She placed the second glass on the ground next to Kret. She then held up her glass to the fallen warlord and took a drink.

"You will never again claim a life in Amon or anywhere else." Kret's body was still. Bren waited for a response, but there was none. "It's customary for the victorious general to say something charitable about the defeated side and its leadership, but I have no kind words for you. And why would I? This was an uncommon war during uncommon times. I think about the people you killed. The cities you razed. The families left to starve. I—" Bren paused. She couldn't think of what else to say. It didn't matter. None of it mattered.

She kicked at the glass on the ground, knocking it over, spilling out the red wine.

* * *

The actor playing Bren held out her glass of wine to the audience. The play was nearing its end, with one more scene after this one.

The sun was lower in the sky. During the previous scene, Pike had placed several lanterns along the edge of the swept stage. The light shone underneath the actor, creating monstrous shadows across her face. The actor playing Kret feigned death, laying on the ground. He faced away from the audience. He tried to not move and kept his breathing as shallow as possible.

Bren paced confidently about the stage, still wearing her armor. Sword sheathed at her side.

"Charitably, I may speak of a foe.

But no kind words for Kret's violence and woe.
An uncommon war of an uncommon age.
I have no words for the unwritten page."

Ekor watched from behind the curtain. He still wore his squirrel suit, even though his part was over. The other players had insisted he wear it during the final dance at the close.

Ekor placed his hand over his mouth as he laughed at these lines about having "no words." This monologue was the longest one in the whole play. The actor had begged to abridge the speech, but Pike insisted every line was crucial.

"—of the people you killed and cities razed.
The families left to starve, half-mad, half-crazed.
Thus, I cannot then speak for the life you stole.
Amon forever torn, no longer whole."

Ekor's focus drifted from the monologue to watch the audience sitting in the grass. Before the play began, they had been so distracted, but now they were all lulled into the magic that theatre works on people. He'd seen this magic almost every night they performed this play and others. Tears in their eyes. Genuine smiles and laughter. Families drew each other closer. It was silly to have people dress in costumes and recite lines, but somehow it all felt real after a while.

Next week, they were to start rehearsals on a new play, the *Princess and the Goblin*. Ekor had been promised the role of the miner's son, which was much better than playing woodland animals. The miner's son stomped on the goblin's oversized feet several times in the play. His favorite part.

"—upon the earth, I hereby pour my draught,
Like the spilt blood stains the earth on behalf
Of farmer and kin, all who doth love life,
Shed by the soldier, cut by the hound's knife."

Bren took the cup next to Kret's body and held it up for the whole audience to see. She then turned it upside down. Even though there wasn't anything in the cup, it represented her pouring it out, and that worked for the play. This action signaled the end of the scene. Jamison, the actor playing Kret, was still wearing stilts wrapped in fur. He got up with the help of the other actor. They then exited the stage. Jamison gave an approving nod to Ekor. He had played his part well, and he felt the energy from it.

Pike pranced onto the stage in long exaggerated strides, ready to give her final monologue and introduce the last scene. She was in a good mood. The war was won. All that remained was for Bren to woo Halsten and Corrinae.

"Vouchsafe to those who do not already know this story, I'll explain it to you," Pike cocked her head back conspiratorially. "Is that what I've been doing this whole time?"

Pike's playful presence was a nice contrast to the battle and famed death monologue. The audience laughed, happy for the change in mood. "But I must apologize. I can't possibly explain everything that happened over the course of Bren's great life. We lack the cast. Our scriptwriter is too lazy, and eventually," Pike gestured to the patron. "You'll need to get back to work." The audience booed at Pike. "What? I'm not the one making you commit to your trade." Pike leaned in. "I'm also not the one paying you. I'm an actor. You pay me. And then I take your coin and do unspeakable things to the young men and women of this village. I encourage them to join me and become actors. It's true. We kidnap people all the time and fill their heads with dreams. It's a dreadful business. I wouldn't recommend it. Cobble shoes instead." To emphasize her point, Pike jumped up and clicked her heels together. "Back to the matter at hand. With no one left to fight, the soldiers were sent to their homes—to rejoice with family and mourn the dead. Bren and a small entourage remain. Let's pick up Bren with our winged thoughts and heave her toward Gandryll. Set her there gently, so she may meet Corrinae and Halsten. Corrinae, you've met. Halsten, we haven't shown him yet. He's part of the happy union too." Pike spun around once and then continued. "The nobles of Gandryll are worried they may lose their heads for treasonous scheming. They hope an advantageous union may save their skin and prevent civil strife with Bren, who has risen like a god over Amon. And now you know all that is worth knowing for us to complete this story. Forgive my abbreviation. Let's return to Gandryll."

Pike blew a kiss and exited, while the actor playing Corrinae, wearing an auburn wig, and the actor playing Halsten, wearing a black wig, walked onto the stage. The auburn wig was long with flowing waves. The black one was also long, but straight, and pulled back into a tight ponytail. These wigs, plus Bren's blonde wig, had been treated like spun gold—carefully groomed, styled, and locked away in a special case. Ekor had been forbidden from even touching the wigs, which always annoyed him because he never even cared about the wigs until he was told he couldn't mess with them. He watched with a certain envy as the actors stroked and primped their hair.

"My father has been killed by the monstrous Kret Bonebreaker," said Corrinae, immediately diving into the character's grief with a loud, wavering voice. "And now, I must endure further torment when the high general comes to Gandryll to exact revenge for treason I did not commit!"

"Or, Corrinae, mayhaps you can soften the heart of a

warrior with your wit and your womanly ways?" Halsten strutted around, indicating a double entendre.

The audience laughed.

"And what of you, good Halsten? Can you work the warrior to our will?" Again, another indecent interpretation as Corrinae gestured to Halsten's crotch when she said "work the warrior." Ekor didn't understand half of it, but the double meanings were there. Corrinae delivered these lines and the debilitating grief from a few seconds ago was forgotten. The dead father would never again come up. Ekor always thought this was odd. This whole scene didn't fit with the story, but everyone wanted a happy end to this story. It must end with a marriage.

"Let us both work and claim a rapturous release from any bondage Bren may have in mind," Halsten said, speaking more to the audience than Corrinae.

"Do you think Bren will bind us with chains?"

"I hope so—" Halsten corrected himself. "I mean, that would be dreadful."

"Will she cuff us to the wall?"

"If we are fortunate. She may have worse in mind."

"Whip us and beat us?" Corrinae emoted.

"Aye, aye!" Halsten was hopeful. "We have been so naughty in our treachery."

"Maybe you have, but my thoughts have been pure. I want nothing but happiness for our Bren. I've worked no treason against her. But quiet—Bren enters my chamber."

The actor playing Bren returned to the stage. No longer dressed in armor, but wearing an elegant gown. This costume change was one of the trickiest, but the transformation was miraculous. Bren was no longer the bruised warrior, but a stunningly beautiful figure. She walked in holding a coil of rope. Corrinae put her hands to her face, fearful of what the rope might mean, while Halsten leapt with excitement about what the rope might mean.

The audience roared with laughter.

"Fair Corrinae, and most fair." Bren softened when she saw Corrinae. Feeling a bit left out, Halsten cleared his throat. Bren corrected herself. "One of the most fair. If the honor is to be shared, both are equally fair."

"Why, Bren, did you bring these bindings into my bedroom?" Corrinae pointed to the rope. Halsten leaned forward.

"Yes, please tell us."

Bren looked at the rope, herself forgetting why she had it. "Oh, this. The people of Eloe Vale have a tradition when pledging fidelity."

Corrinae looked pleased with the answer. Halsten, disappointed.

"And how does this tradition work?" Corrinae asked.

"It's simple." Bren handed one end of the rope to Corrinae and Halsten, looping the rope once, then twice around each hand, while she held the other end and looped it twice as well. "When we are joined thusly, we can only speak true. To do otherwise would be to invite calamity upon ourselves. In this moment, we would profess a commitment of family forever bonded in matrimony."

"Bren, you move too quickly." Corrinae uncoiled the rope from her hands. "I'm not ready for such a promise."

Halsten pulled Corrinae aside.

"Are you mad?" Halsten hissed at her. "This is the very thing we've wanted. Let's get to the point. The bed of marriage will groan under our weight, whether it be night or day! And being so, let's not delay."

"The tongues of warriors are full of deceit," Corrinae responded. "Such people will say whatever to claim their territory. In the War of the Hounds, what spoils could Bren claim? She cannot lay with a dog. No heir can be produced. So, instead, she must turn to those who supported Kret, even if that support came under duress. If we are to form a union, willful but consenting, an enemy turned friend and ally, it must mean something—or else, we are indentured servants. It does us no good to be plowed in the field and then have the harvest rot on the vine."

"Did thou speak of plowing?" Bren asked, overhearing them.

"Yes," Corrinae responded. "No," Halsten said at the same time. They looked at each other and then both switched their responses.

"Gentle Corrinae, do not presume on my forthrightness," Bren approached Corrinae. "I take your hand, not your yoke. Your beauty—" Again, Halsten cleared his throat. "And your beauty as well. Both are beautiful in my eyes as I have two eyes with each of you set in them."

Ekor shook his head as he watched. He never understood this part of the play. It made no sense for Bren Caius to become so smitten with two people she had just met, and especially to marry them. It all moved too fast. That's how it was with these plays. Always one character who was overeager and the other resistant, but the resistant one would give in after hearing the right words.

"You have one heart. Is it enough for both of us?" Corrinae placed her hand on Bren and kept her at a distance.

"My heart pumps blood to all my extremities. Just as my love can reach out in several directions." Bren placed her hand under Corrinae's chin, lifting it to better meet her gaze. Then Bren reached out to Halsten, bringing him close with her other hand. "I have one hand to pluck a flower, but two lovers won't be a problem, because I can deflower with two hands."

The audience laughed. Ekor decided he had enough of the play and walked back to join the other actors who were waiting for the final dance.

Mikkel, who often played the Fool, was cast as one of the nobles for this play. He was still wearing his finery, but had removed the dark red leather gloves. He held a pheasant plume, running it along his fingers and waving it about.

"The audience is laughing, Master Ekor," Mikkel mused. "And yet, you seemed bored. Did we fail to entertain you tonight?"

"No," Ekor sat on one of the crates. "I just think this scene is dumb."

"Everyone thinks it's dumb." Mikkel waved the plume at Ekor, who swatted it away. "That's why they're laughing."

Ekor rolled his eyes. Mikkel put a hand on Ekor's shoulder.

"None of that, young player. You're not better than us. This is what we do. This is the job. You wear the squirrel outfit with pride." Mikkel waved the feather over Ekor. "The true story of what happened to Bren, Corrinae, and Halsten is too tragic to share."

This caught Ekor's attention.

"What happened?"

"No one knows for certain, but this is what I heard." Mikkel paused as the audience on the other side of the curtain laughed at something in the play itself, then continued. "After the final battle, Bren arrived in Gandryll as a person hollowed out, empty. Something happened that shook her, even more than the battle itself. She was drained and had no interest in politics or any penitence the nobility could throw at her. Corrinae and Halsten showed great care and patience. Bren knew that a union would satisfy the nobility and prevent future conflict. But in the end, a loveless marriage is a loveless marriage. Corrinae and Halsten had each other, and no one had Bren Caius. They followed her back to Rhyll. They adopted and raised Mendal Caius, but Bren's fiery spirit had died that evening after the battle in Pynne's Field. All that remained was a ghost and the stories of who she once was."

"And no one knows what happened after the final battle?" Ekor asked.

"It's a true mystery." Mikkel placed the plume in his velvet flat cap and admired it. "You don't have many of those. Usually, someone has a theory. But at this specific moment, there's silence about what happened." Ekor's head filled with questions, but he couldn't put them together into words. Mikkel placed his hat on his head. "Come on, young player. Let's get in position. The play's almost over."

Corrinae, moved by Bren's words about how "customs curtsy to greatness," stepped forward to embrace Bren, but Halsten, also moved, moved for Bren at the same time. They collided and knocked the blonde wig off the high general. This physical comedy was planned, but the audience howled with laughter at the absurdity of this accident. Corrinae and Halsten bent over to grab Bren's wig and once again collided. This time, they knocked off their auburn and black wigs. More laughter. The three loves all bent over for a third collision. They grabbed a wig and promptly put it on their heads. They stood up, confident all was well. The wigs were in disarray—sideways on Bren, backwards on Halsten, and upside down on Corrinae. And most unfortunate of all, they were each wearing the wrong one. Their eyes went wide with the horror of their mistake. People in the audience were on their sides, falling on each other, rolling with laughter. After such a long play about the terrors of war and the burden of leadership, they needed something to laugh about.

The actors grabbed for each other's wigs, but once again, they had the wrong one on their head. What came next was a flurry of grabbing at wigs, moving from one head to the next—a juggling act of sorts, as the auburn, blonde, and black wigs went around and around. The actors became increasingly flustered.

Pike walked onto the stage and yelled, "Stop!"

She went to Bren and shoved the blonde wig into her hands. She gave Corrinae the auburn wig. She gave Halsten his black wig. They sheepishly fixed them on their heads. Pike nodded approval and left again.

This time, Corrinae more carefully approached Bren and gave her a kiss. Then Halsten did the same. The audience applauded at the confused threesome figuring it all out.

Bren held out her arms in triumph and gave her final line.

"Then shall I swear to you Corrinae—" Halsten cleared his throat, prompting Bren to not forget him, "—and Halsten, and you both to me, and may our oaths well-kept and prosperous be!"

The three actors took a bow and their wigs fell off again. In unison, they shrugged their shoulders. The rest of the cast joined them on stage. Some people in the audience started playing a lively tune on their lutes, flutes, and bodhrán drums. Everyone clapped to the beat. The actors stomped and spun around, joining hands in a dance where they weaved in and out of the two lines they had formed. After going through the steps twice, they invited everyone else to stand and join them.

The music and dancing continued late into the night, even after the actors had retreated backstage, packing up for their journey to the next village.

* * *

Bren kicked at the glass on the ground and spilled the red wine on the floor. Yulie moved to clean it up, but Bren held out her hand to stop her.

"It's okay. Leave it."

Yulie screamed, the piercing scream only a terrified child could make.

Hild immediately stood up.

Ruth, with the dead mouse in her talons, flew from her perch and out of the tent.

Bren looked around to see what was happening. Yulie pointed past Bren to Kret's body. The girl shook all over like a baby calf standing for the first time. Bren slowly turned around to see Kret's chest raising and lowering. He was breathing. The wound was smaller than before. It was closing up.

"This demon is not done with us," Hild said.

Kret, not fully conscious, groaned as life returned to him. The sense of dread overwhelmed Bren. This dread could only be compared to things she had never experienced but could easily imagine—the feeling of treading water in the middle of the ocean, no shore and no ship in sight; the feeling of being trapped deep within the earth and unable to claw your way out; the feeling of falling from a mountain cliff as the rocky ground fast approached.

Bren's throat tightened as though she were being choked. She could barely stand.

Kret lived, though she had killed him. She had driven her sword through his chest, and it wasn't enough.

Bren could only stare at Kret's body and wait for whatever would happen next. Her skin warmed and prickled. She felt an intense pressure on the back of her head, a pulsing ache that seemed to come from nowhere. Her vision narrowed. She had faced a troll in combat once. It felt like this.

Bren did not have the strength to fight Kret again. If he couldn't be killed, if he kept coming back, the fight would never end. She would never be free. The fear reminded her of when she was a child seeing a chaotic world through the eyes of every wild beast. It was the feeling that this topsy-turvy moment would be her life forever. It wasn't death that scared her. It was the lack of control. Another scream from Yulie broke the spell.

"Yulie! Quiet!"

The girl flinched as though she had been slapped. The celebratory noises outside had ceased. Someone would be in here soon to check on Bren.

She couldn't kill Kret, but she could contain him. She needed to regain control.

Bren grabbed Kret, wrapping her arms around him and lifting him up. His skin was warm. Hild joined Bren. They both grunted as they dragged him toward the arcane crate. They did not have the strength to lift him any farther off the ground. Bren took a deep breath and tried again, pulling from some strength she didn't know she had. Bren and Hild were able to get him halfway into the crate. Then Bren grabbed his legs and lifted them up and over into the crate. Kret flopped into it. Bren reached for the lid of the crate. The runes glowed at her touch, and she slammed the lid down.

Before it closed, Kret's hand reached out and grabbed Bren's wrist. His claws dug into her skin, drawing blood. She tried to pull free, but he was too strong.

"Bren?" Kret asked. He was dazed, but the malice in his voice was still there. "Death can't keep me away from you. I'll always come back."

Kret let go, allowing her to shut the lid. The runes pulsed for a moment and then faded. Only Bren would be able to open it again.

"You must tell no one about what has happened," Hild spoke with a confidence and authority that unnerved Bren. "Oren will be in here soon. You must lie to him."

"But why? He should know."

"Tell no one," Hild glared at Bren. "You must have faith that this guidance does not come from me, but the goddess who saved you today."

"I'm not doing anything just because you think Tian speaks to you," Bren responded brusquely, but she knew there was some truth to the priest's words. Oren would never accept a Kret that couldn't be killed. He would fight and fight until there was nothing left. And maybe that was the right answer, but Bren needed time and space to think. She couldn't tell him the truth, at least not yet.

Oren burst into the tent, carrying his sheathed sword with him. He had rushed here and did not even bother to draw his sword. Oren looked around, unsure if he had actually heard screaming from the tent.

"Bren, what happened?" His tone was threatening. He was ready, always ready, to attack.

Bren looked at Hild and then Yulie. The poor child was terrified, and she had every reason to be.

Bren did not know what to say. She was lost within her tangled thoughts. What would she do about Kret? There was a dragon pit underneath the palace in Rhyll and a cage with adamantine steel bars. The palace and the dragon pit were a gift from the previous elven occupants—built a thousand years before humans migrated to Amon. If the cage could hold a small dragon, it could hold Kret. It might work.

"What happened?" Oren asked again.

"The goblin war mage Speck teleported here and then disappeared with Kret's body," Hild spoke for Bren. "He brought a troll with him, but Bren was able to seal the troll in this crate before his hypnotic powers took effect. We were lucky."

"Why would Speck steal Kret's body?" Oren was dubious of this story.

"To prevent us from parading Kret's corpse through Amon?" Bren fumbled through her words. "I don't know. Pride? For whatever reason, he didn't want us to have the body."

"Can you use Ruth to scout for Speck and follow him? Like you did before."

"I can't," Bren hesitated. "He's—just gone."

"And we have a troll in there?" Oren pointed to the arcane crate with his sword.

"Yes," Hild said.

Oren tried his best to arrive at a solution. "Let's grab a torch, some lamp oil, and drop it in the crate. Light the troll up."

"No." Bren sounded guilty, and Oren knew something was awry. "I'd like to take this crate back to Rhyll. We'll study this troll. I'd like to learn more about the magical effect of these creatures. We'll face them again at some point. We can be better prepared."

Oren knew Bren and Hild were lying, but they were united in holding onto this lie. Oren would have to accept what he was given.

Yulie started to cry. She did not want to be part of it.

"You can't tell anyone what happened," Bren said to Yulie. Her voice was uncharacteristically high pitched, filled with desperation and pleading. "You must keep this secret for the rest of your life. There is no one you can confide in, not ever— on penalty of death. Do you understand?"

Yulie nodded as she cried. The crying of a child was so distinct, wholly unlike anything else—certainly not like an adult crying. Bren would know. She had reduced many people to tears. She was familiar with the blubbering of drunks, the grieving homesick soldier, the rejected and abandoned friend, Owyn Oldcastle.

The sound of Yulie crying would stay with Bren forever. After this evening, if she ever heard a child cry, it would hit Bren hard, catching her unprepared. She would need to excuse herself from the room and start crying as well. It unlocked something in her, twisted and damaged. Guilt unending. She would never heal. She did not want to heal or be forgiven.

Oren placed his sword on the ground. He reached for Yulie, placed his hand on her neck and snapped it. All sound from Yulie ceased with a short gasp. She dropped lifeless to the ground.

Yulie did not move. Her red curls fanned out around her.

"What did you do?" Bren's voice shook softly.

"I did what you would never be able to do," Oren said with such ease and strange indifference. Bren hated him. "A child could never keep such a secret. I can. Your priest can. But with a little girl, it would get out. And you're right. Whatever secret you're keeping," Oren eyed the arcane crate. "It must stay a secret."

"But—" Bren couldn't finish her words. She was still expecting Yulie to stand up again, but she would not.

Bren felt cold.

She screamed at Oren. She hit him across the face. Oren stood firm and took the hit. She hit him again and again until his face broke and bled, as did her hand. She pounded at his chest. He stood as a stone statue.

"I did what had to be done."

"No! No, that's absurd! I refuse to accept that!"

More soldiers congregated outside the tent flap, talking among themselves if they should enter. Bren yelled at them, "Stay out there!"

Bren glared at Oren with raw hatred. If she had her sword in hand, she would have killed him. But already, the scene within the tent was too difficult to explain. "Oren, leave me, you broken thing, you wasted vessel. I never want to see you again. I command you to take your own life."

"I won't," Oren said.

"I command you!" Bren hit him again. Blood ran down his face.

"You will forgive me. One day, you'll call me back to your side."

"Oren speaks truth," Hild said.

Bren had nothing left in her. She fell to her knees and screamed again. She pressed her face to the ground, near the spilt wine, and screamed. Oren left the tent and muttered to curious soldiers to scatter. There was an accident, too much wine, but all would be well.

"This is what needed to happen." Hild's voice was quiet, barely above a rustling breeze. "The child wouldn't be able to keep such a secret."

"Who *are* you?"

"I am who you needed." Hild's hair turned gray as she spoke. "And I am no one." Deeper lines formed at the corners of her eyes. Her eyes sunk inward. Her cheeks drooped. Her dragon sigil tattoo faded. Hild withered into a skinnier, frailer form.

Hild looked at her wrinkled hands, amazed but not surprised.

"I've been serving Tian for many centuries." Hild smiled. "And now my time is over. We should all be so fortunate to grow old." With those words, Hild disappeared.

Bren was dumbfounded. Everything had happened too quickly, and she did not understand what was going on. All that mattered was the girl's body on the ground. Bren crawled over to her, crying her name over and over again.

Yulie had a mother once. The gnolls had killed her whole family, but she had a mother. Bren thought of this woman whom she didn't know. Yulie had survived. She was meant to live and continue their family's memory, but now that memory was lost forever.

"Death, unfairly and untimely, awarded to your dearest darling." Bren spoke to no one, an unintelligible mumbling. "The child you grew within you. Little more than a seed, the tiniest unspoiled fruit, plucked from the vine, your womb. You birthed her and fed her. You cared for her through long nights and early mornings. You held her close until she went to sleep, and you dreamed for her. You dreamed of a life—filled with kindness and gentleness, and love—a life that belonged solely to your child, and I cut it short. Dashing the fruit upon the ground. Damn me to the hells. Her death will preserve the lie. But why? Because a priest said so? This was unnecessary. Outside this tent, soldiers are celebrating my valor. But I'm no hero—I am—"

Bren thought of Hild. She was gone. Were the gods now silent as well?

Bren thought of Aubec—a good man, but one she could never trust again, not after he betrayed their confidence to the nobles of Gandryll. She would keep him at Sage Hall, near, but always at arm's length.

She thought of Oren, and it pained her. In many ways, he was the opposite of Aubec. He was loyal, trustworthy, but he was not a good man. And lastly, she thought of Owyn Oldcastle and how she walked past him, pretending she didn't know him—and how that must have ruined him.

Bren whispered, "I am alone."

She heard a low voice from within the crate.

Kret was speaking, but she could not make out the words. She crawled closer and put her ear against the cold wall of the casket.

Kret spoke again. "You don't know much about me."

"And you know too much about me."

"I go by many names, but my oldest name is Cerneboch. I was born when the tree of life first sprouted. I came into existence as the counterbalance. I cannot be killed."

Bren gave a weak, empty laugh. "Now you tell me."

"You cannot starve me, drown me, burn me, or bury me. If you destroy my body, my spirit will roam this wide world until it finds new flesh."

"You're a demon."

"Oppose me and I become stronger."

"Tough talk for someone trapped in a box."

"You were a worthy adversary. You just didn't know what you were up against."

Bren closed her eyes as she spoke. "Why were you ordering your legion to cut down certain trees?"

Kret paused. He chose his words carefully, not wanting to reveal too much. "There is another war happening, beyond this world, a war among named gods and spirits and fey and dragons. And we all have a part to play. This is mine."

Bren leaned against the crate for some time. She kept her eyes closed, not wanting to look at the girl's broken body. Bren thought about the story of Vorghenmauller, the dragon who ate the children of the village. What did it matter if the knight was brave, especially when everyone else was so willing to sacrifice the children to save themselves?

Eventually, Bren broke the long silence.

"When you first spoke, I couldn't hear what you were saying. What was it?"

"I said, 'You're not alone.'" His words were both smug and threatening. "You have me."

Perhaps the lanterns were low on oil. The flames faded to pinpricks and then into nothing. Behind closed eyes, Bren felt a greater darkness. A complete darkness, only possible in the deepest caverns. She wanted to dive into this oblivion and float along the barren landscapes of a world—dark, indifferent, and vast. The darkness was unnatural, and like so many exceptional things, it could not last.

* * *

Corrinae and Halsten sat at a table in the solar, waiting for Bren Caius to arrive. The solar was a smaller room on the second floor, not normally used for entertaining guests. The room was for the leisurely and informal gatherings of family and friends. Corrinae felt this cozy room would send the message that Bren Caius was no normal visitor. The room included a fireplace on one end, as well as decorative woodwork and tapestries hanging along the walls. Opposite the fireplace were the largest shuttered windows in the manor. When opened, they let in the most sunlight, especially in the spring and fall.

The bench across from Corrinae and Halsten was empty.

They knew Bren Caius was in the city. They had received confirmation she would arrive this afternoon, and there had been no updates or changes in the plan. Bren was late, or perhaps she wasn't coming. The wait was agonizing.

Corrinae and Halsten heard the front door open from downstairs. Both sat up straight and smoothed out the wrinkles in their clothing.

An indiscernible voice spoke to their doorman—a rude rambling of apologies and excuses. The ramblings grew louder as Corrinae and Halsten heard footsteps on the stairs. Halsten gave Corrinae's hand a squeeze.

Bren Caius pushed past the doorman who had guided her to the second floor. Bren stumbled into the room. She reeked of what Corrinae could only describe as tavern smells. The doorman rushed forward to pull out the bench for Bren, but she pushed him away. She sat down, nearly missing the bench entirely. Everyone stood up in a panic that she might fall over, but Bren steadied herself. Once Bren was confident that the bench would not betray her and that she was firmly situated, she looked over at Corrinae and Halsten. Bren's eyes were red and sunken. Her hair clung to her sweaty face. If it weren't for the finely tooled leather scabbard on her hip with the sheathed sword, Corrinae would think they'd invited a vagrant into their home.

Corrinae and Halsten each forced a smile. In unison, they grabbed for their cups and took a sip. Bren surveyed the room, unable to focus on any single thing.

"Can I get you some tea?" Corrinae asked, urging decorum. Inside, Corrinae was a wreck. Bren Caius wasn't the strong, graceful knight Corrinae had hoped for.

Bren snorted at the suggestion of tea, but no one else got the joke.

"I'm fine," Bren lied. "Which one of you is Corrinae and which one is Halsten? I've been told that a union between our houses would appease the nobles. I get you on your back. I keep the nobles off my back. Is that how it works?"

Corrinae held back her tears at Bren's crassness. Halsten took the lead.

"This is Corrinae of Umber. I'm Halsten of Cain-Oldcastle. I believe you knew my uncle, Owyn?" The name caught Bren's attention, but she did not respond. After a long silence,

Halsten continued. "Is there anyone else we might know from House Caius?"

Bren slapped the table. Cups rattled. "I'm a house of one. It's just me and my name, which your uncle paid for."

"A good investment."

"He did it because I'm Bren the Beloved. I'm beloveable." The word stumped Bren. It felt like it should be a word, but it didn't sound right. "I'm Bren the Beloved." She said it again.

"Yes," Halsten said unsteadily. "I must congratulate you on an impressive victory in Pynne's Field. In a few days, we'd like to host a feast at the manor celebrating your many accomplishments during the war."

"I'm leaving tonight for Rhyll. I have an important item to deliver."

"Oh." Corrinae could not decide if she was disappointed or relieved by this news. "Will you be returning to Gandryll?"

"No, you'll come with me. I'm sure you have people who pack your things when you need to travel. Let them know."

Unprompted, Bren stood up, knocking into the table. The cups fell over. Halsten and Corrinae grabbed their napkins to clean up the spill. Bren stumbled back a few steps and then unsheathed her sword, pointing it at the fireplace. The sword dripped with blood.

"Dear me!" Corrinae grabbed Halsten's shoulder, unsure what else to do.

Bren was confused at Corrinae's reaction. She then looked at her sword. "Oh, sorry." Bren grabbed the tablecloth and wiped off the blood. "Sorry. Before I came here, I had to deal with some traitors. Aubec," Bren tapped her sword along the stone outer wall. "He wouldn't tell me who they were, but I took care of it."

Corrinae's heart sunk. "How did you . . . ?"

"You might be the only nobles left in Gandryll. You're a house of one." Bren pointed her sword at Halsten. "And you're a house of one." Bren pointed her sword at Corrinae. "Except we can't find Tomas. Maybe you're a house of two?"

"You're a monster." Corrinae wept as she spoke. Her face was broken with grief.

"No, I'm a high general. You'll join me in Rhyll. We don't need to have a happy union or even a consummated one. It's all theatre, anyway. Just let the other nobles in Amon know that the matter has been settled. Debts are paid. Wrongs have been addressed. All is forgiven. For now."

"You're a monster!" Corrinae screamed as Halsten held her.

Bren walked away from the table and back into the hallway —swinging her sword as she went, but with no one left to fight.

ACKNOWLEDGMENTS

To Holly Lyn Walrath, Tricia Klapprodt, and Kara Robinson, my wonderful editors, who give me what every author desperately needs: clarity and direction,

To Jarrett Rush and Matt Cobb who meet with me almost every Wednesday to talk about writing and publishing,

To Daniel Irving Decena who illustrated this cover,

To Francesca Baerald who created the Amon map,

To the independent bookstores and libraries that saved some shelf space for my first fantasy novel,

To Aaron Glover at the Writer's Garret, Blake Kimzey at WritingWorkshops.com, and to all the Shakespearean academics and actors who helped shape my understanding of the Warlike Harry,

To B.S.H. Garcia for her encouraging words,

To Petrik Leo, Kay's Hidden Shelf, SFF Addicts Podcast, Bookborn, David W. Walters, Jr., Aaron M. Payne of Biblio-Theory, Boe Kelley of SFF Insiders, Matthew Sorenson aka Beard of Darkness, Tiny Elf Arcanist, Sarah the Book Fairy, Liv C, and Medieval Ashley,

To the many authors who have inspired me with their audacity and endless hope that the words will somehow come together and tell a story—I can't list everyone, but if you think I'm talking about you, I am,

To my Patreon team Tad Lake, Erin Taylor, Bob Moser, Erkan & Caitlin Eyvaz, Paul Milligan, Josh Rose, Gian Cruz, Jolyn Redden, Daniel Miller, J. Kyle Fagan, Alyssa Sable, Brian Johnson, Kacie & Evan Elwood, Tonya & Jay Rosenberger, Nancy & Randy Hopkins, Rachel Lane, Shelby Cunningham, Jesse Sowell, Carl Walter, and Pat Hauldren,

To the music I listened to while writing these books, in particular: Sam Lee, Aurora, Apashe, Myrkur, and Wardruna,

To Maryam Baig, Dan Hughes, Curtis Glenn, Chris "Waffles" Wathen, Sean Carpentier, Michael Brown, Brad McEntire, and my sister Lizz,

To my amazing daughters Kennedy and Greta,

And to my wife April, you are "my perpetual idea" (Sorolla).

A special thank you to the beta-readers: Finley James and Justin Greer

ABOUT THE AUTHOR

David Hopkins is a fantasy author. His short stories have been featured in Infinite Worlds, Oni Press, and Image Comics. He's created a few best-selling "Red War" titles for the D&D Adventurers League, and he's written stories for a variety of magazines and newspapers.

David is a member of SFWA (Science Fiction and Fantasy Writers Association) and teaches classes through WritingWorkshops.com. He's married to artist, April Hopkins. They have two daughters, Kennedy and Greta, and a dog named Moose.

Visit thatdavidhopkins.com for updates on the series and exclusive bonus material.

ALSO FROM DAVID HOPKINS

Four titans sleep beneath the earth. Only one fae can keep them from waking.

Silbrey is an orphaned wood nymph, taken from her forest home and raised in the corrupt city of Penderyn. The fae child grows up unaware of who she is, what she can do, and the calling of her kind.

Under the control of a cruel guildmaster, Silbrey is trained as an assassin. As an adult, she escapes her violent past to start a new life and a family. But a tragic death brings her back to the familiar cobbled streets to seek revenge. This dark path leads Silbrey to uncover an even darker secret: An ancient evil will wake the titans and break the world. Silbrey must travel with her daughter across a war-torn land to defeat that evil.

What begins as a fairy tale transforms into a multi-generational epic fantasy about love and loss—and a woman with a strange connection to nature.

Visit www.DryadsCrown.com to order the ebook, paperback, or audiobook.

"A library is a focal point, a sacred place to a community; and its sacredness is its accessibility, its publicness. It's everybody's place."
– Ursula K. Le Guin

Unite Against Book Bans is a national campaign to protect the rights of everyone to access a variety of books, in libraries and elsewhere.

- Books are tools for understanding complex issues.
- Young people deserve to see themselves reflected in a library's books.
- Parents should not be making decisions for other parents' children.
- Individuals should be trusted to make their own decisions about what to read.
- Limiting young people's access to books does not protect them from life's complex and challenging issues.

Support the freedom to read. Oppose book bans.
Visit UniteAgainstBookBans.org

www.ingramcontent.com/pod-product-compliance
Lightning Source LLC
Chambersburg PA
CBHW011431310726
48972CB00011B/3009